Doom Buggy

A Sammy & Brian Mystery #5

By Ken Munro

Gaslight Publishers

Gaslight Publishers
P. O. Box 258
Bird-in-Hand, PA 17505

Library of Congress Number: 96-79958
International Standard Book Number: 1-883294-48-7
Cover designed by Marshall's Graphics, Elverson, Pa.

Printed by
Masthof Press
Route 1, Box 20, Mill Road
Morgantown, PA 19543-9701

DEDICATION

This book is for
Arianna Kathleen
my granddaughter.

Special thanks to
Corporal Marlene Leighty
Leonard McChesney
and Tim Hoerner.

Also special thanks to
my daughters, Kim, Joyce and Karen,
and sons-in-law, Marc, Wilson and Ben,
for their valuable editing and suggestions.

Help Sammy and Brian discover the message contained in these letters.

Cut out the twenty letters below and rearrange them into words. If you form the correct words, they will form a sentence, revealing an important message. (You must use all of the letters.)

i	u	w	h
o	y	l	e
l	y	d	r
i	n	u	p
o	i	o	s

CHAPTER ONE

B rian Helm's eyes closed and his face wrinkled. "This is going to be the dumb-est case we ever worked on." Having said that, he opened his eyes and waited for a reaction from his friend, Sammy Wilson, and Sammy's uncle who were about to enter Amishman David Fisher's carriage shop.

Ron Williams, Sammy's uncle, winked at his nephew and turned to face Brian. "If by *dumbest* you mean this case is going to be *easy*, then good. You two amateur detectives can have the case solved by the end of the day. Dave will appreciate that."

Brian frowned. "It's just dumb, that's all. Why would anyone want to steal an Amish buggy?"

"That's why we're offering our services to Mr. Fisher," answered Sammy. "We're going to find out."

"I bet some kids drove by in a truck late at night," said Brian. "They spotted the buggy sitting here in front of the shop. The one kid says, 'Hey, let's have some fun.' He jumps into the back of the truck, grabs the buggy, and they drive off. They pull the buggy behind them, up and down the back roads. On top of a hill they let it go. Then they get their kicks from watching the buggy roll backwards down the hill and crash into a tree."

"Brian, it's been three days," said Sammy. "The police have already scoured these back roads." He smiled and added, "And nobody has reported seeing a buggy *wrapped around a tree*."

Brian's face went into neutral as he searched for an answer to redeem himself. "I know," he said as his finger stabbed at the air. "The buggy missed the tree, went over a bank, and sank in the creek. It's now hidden under ten feet of water." His mouth closed, producing a smile.

Sammy and his uncle just glanced at each other and shook their heads.

"What? What?" asked Brian as the door opened and he followed Sammy and his uncle into David Fisher's carriage shop.

The Amish carriage shop was located across the road from Ron Williams' farm. When David Fisher bought and moved into the non-Amish farm, the first thing he did was rip out all the electrical wiring. He replaced the furnace, pumps, stoves, and lights, operated by electricity, with appliances operated by compressed air and propane gas. He then insulated the barn and covered it inside and out with tin. It now operated as a carriage shop, producing Amish buggies—*but not for the taking.*

David Fisher had mentioned the missing buggy to Ron Williams. Ron had mentioned it to his nephew. Sammy of course had told his best friend, Brian. And Brian? Well, he had just thrown up his hands and exclaimed, "A buggy? Who would want to steal an Amish buggy?"

"Hey, David," yelled Ron, closing the door behind them. "It's Ron. Are you here?"

"Wait, onct," came a faint voice from below.

Sammy's uncle had been in the carriage shop before, but this was the first time for the young detectives. Sammy looked around and saw no one. The interior of the shop was hot and stuffy. Opened windows allowed fresh air to venture inside the converted barn, but they certainly didn't act as a cooling system. Several gas lanterns hung from the corrugated metal ceiling. These lanterns supplied needed light when the Amishman worked into the night.

Instead of electric wires, air hoses meandered over the ceiling and down the walls. A generator out back, run by diesel fuel, produced compressed air that operated all of David's tools. Even the sewing machine, used to stitch the gray canvas outer covering of the buggies and its upholstery, was run by a compressed air motor.

The main floor of the shop held several carriages in various stages of construction. Two rectangular bodies, framed with wood and fiber-glass, were ready to be covered with canvas. The springs and metal frames that held the body were on the floor waiting to be fitted with a hydraulic brake system.

Brian noted an Interstate battery dealership sign nailed to the wall. Beneath, on a rack, were several automobile batteries. A carriage shop was the last place Brian expected to find car batteries.

Sammy noticed Brian's quizzical expression. "The car batteries are used for the warning lights on the buggies."

Now Brian was really confused. "Well, how do they recharge the batteries if they don't use electricity?"

Ron Williams smiled. "The Amish use the diesel generator to charge the batteries."

"But, doesn't the generator produce..." Brian's words trailed off. He thought he better not pursue the matter. Anyway he noticed something more interesting: a tall wrought iron rack that held large rolls of fabric. The curious teenager wondered whether Amish cloth was different from "regular" cloth. He strolled over and rubbed his hand over a bolt of material. "Clink, clank, clunk," screeched the rack. The fabric flapped and started to unravel, curling up on the floor four feet beneath.

Brian, overreacting, hurled his body against the rotating cloth, trying to stop it. But the fabric, already on the floor, caused his foot to slip. His arms flailed in the air and he lost his balance. "Help! Help!" he yelled and landed beneath the cascading fabric.

"What's wrong?" shouted Sammy as he and his uncle rushed toward the muffled cries for help. While Ron's arms clamped around the spinning roll of cloth, Sammy reached for a leg and pulled his friend from the mound of cloth.

"Brian, what were you doing?" asked Sammy, helping his friend to his feet.

Brian coughed and released the last of the cloth from around his face. "I was investigating part of the shop here. You know, trying to get the feel of the carriage business. And I can tell you something."

"Yeah, what's that?" asked Sammy.

"Amish cloth feels the same as regular cloth; however, it's more aggressive." He smiled to cover his embarrassment.

As the three rewrapped the cloth back onto the roll, they heard a rumble coming from below the far left corner of the room. Brian's heartbeat quickened as he slid behind his partner. He poked his head out to see what kind of creature was invading the carriage shop.

Ron just smiled at the teenagers who watched in amazement as a head, wearing a straw hat, slowly appeared from beneath the floor. The head focused on the boys and spoke. "You weren't expecting to see an elevator in an Amish barn, yah?"

The rest of David Fisher's body gradually appeared at floor level. Sammy smiled and stepped aside, exposing Brian, not to a monster of the deep, but to a lone Amishman standing on the movable floor section. Even Sammy was surprised. The elevator was large enough to transport a carriage from one level of the shop to the other.

Sammy glanced up at the air-operated mechanism that supplied power to the elevator. The air motor turned a large gear that was attached to an axle. The axle itself ran across the ceiling directly over the floor opening. Two wire cables, attached to opposite sides of the lift, wrapped around the turning axle, enabling the elevator to rise.

Ron, who was entertained by the boys' reaction to the elevator, stepped forward. "Dave, I have to leave right away, but this is my nephew, Sammy Wilson, and his friend, Brian Helm. They would like to help you find your missing buggy." And with that, he hurried out the door and headed across the road to his house.

David stepped from the elevator. He was twenty-eight, short, skinny, and shy. The clothes he wore were plain and simple. Black cotton pants were supported by suspenders over a pastel purple shirt. His thin face wore a beard, indicating he was married. The Amishman tilted his head, topped by the wide-brimmed straw hat, and squinted his left eye. "Your uncle always hurries about so. It wonders me if he'll ever get there."

Sammy smiled at the Amishman's response then said, "For my uncle, the fun is in the getting."

David nodded his head and glanced at Brian. "You like to get things, too, like the buggy?"

Brian stood tall, nodded his head, and tried to look important. "How deep are the creeks around here?" he asked.

Sammy poked his elbow against his partner's arm. "We've never tried to find a missing buggy before."

"It's the strangest thing," said the Amishman. "I thought some young folks took it for funin' and left it hereabouts."

"That's exactly what—" started Brian.

"But, that way I don't think anymore," continued David. "It's more than horseplay."

Brian was perplexed. He glanced at Sammy, trying to read his reaction to what David was saying. Then, tugging at his jeans and sniffing as though he detected an important clue, he said, "Yeah, it just might be a professional job."

Sammy frowned. "Can you tell us how the buggy was taken?"

Very calmly the Amishman started to explain. For having a buggy stolen, David didn't appear to be upset or anxious. He stated in a matter-of-fact way that the buggy belonged to Amos Zook. Zook had brought in his carriage to have the upholstery replaced. When David had finished the work, he had parked the buggy in front of the shop. That was Friday. Early Saturday morning David had discovered the buggy missing.

"And you didn't see or hear anything during the night?" asked Sammy.

The Amishman shook his head.

Sammy went to a back window and looked down. A small creek ran behind the shop beyond a small parking area. "And you checked with Amos Zook to see if he had picked up the buggy without telling you?"

This time David nodded his head.

"Maybe one of your Amish friends borrowed the buggy," said Brian.

"They wouldn't do that. Not without saying."

Sammy was thinking of other possibilities. "Has anyone come into your shop and shown an interest in buying a carriage?"

"Ah, you want to know suspects." The Amishman rubbed his whiskers, glanced toward a back window, and pointed. "A boy lives back yonder. Name's Barry Bitner. He don't behave good sometimes. He stole some lumber from Mike Herr up the road last month.

Brian strolled to the window. The view was blocked by a hill and trees that followed the stream. He saw nothing useful. So that his actions appeared productive, he puckered his lips and nodded his head. He had seen a detective do that in a movie.

Sammy observed Brian's body language and smiled. He had seen the same movie. Still grinning, he flipped open his note pad, labeled the new page SUSPECTS, and wrote the name Barry Bitner. "Anybody else?" he asked.

"An antique dealer comes here still. He doesn't look so good in the face."

"Do you know his name?" asked Sammy as he prepared to write the second suspect's name.

"Come. I have cards over here in my desk." David took a few steps, yanked on a drawer, and pulled out a handful of business cards. "Here it is. Name is Wally Mills."

Sammy wrote the name and address. "Maybe if you look through the rest of those cards, we can come up with more suspects."

David glanced at the next card. "Alcx Austin. She's doing herself up a restaurant. She wanted a buggy to show good out front for the tourists."

"Alex? I thought Alex was a man's name" said Brian.

"You ever hear the name Alexandra?" asked Sammy.

Brian's face lit up. "Oh, yeah, a woman's name. Alex for short."

"But Alex didn't buy a buggy?" said Sammy in the form of a question.

"No. She didn't have the money right off," said David, still leafing through the remaining cards. "And that's all. The rest are wholesale salesmen cards."

A glint appeared in Sammy's blue eyes. "A salesman might see how easy it would be to steal a buggy. Any salesmen show an interest in your buggies?"

The Amishman placed the cards back into the drawer, giving himself time to think. "Can't rightly think of any."

Small pieces of cut paper on the desk caught Sammy's eye. His curiosity was aroused as he noticed each square contained a letter of the alphabet. "What are those?" he asked as he pointed to the mixture of letters.

y   w   d R   o

l   e   n   s   y   i

o   h   i   P   o   u

i   u   l

"Ach, just such stuff I picked out front off the ground. Been trying to cipher what they spell."

Brian's face perked up as he took a peek. "You think it's a puzzle of some kind?"

"I don't know," said the Amishman. "The wife and I was funin' some with them awhile back. All I know, they spell a handful of words."

"Probably some kid dropped them on the way to school," said Brian. His thumb shot up to his right. "Isn't there a one-room school up the road here?"

David Fisher nodded his head.

Brian picked up two of the letters and examined them. "There's printing on both sides. These were cut from a magazine." He looked at Sammy. "Do you know what those letters are?" asked Brian. "A ransom note. Only the letters aren't glued on a sheet of paper. Hey, the buggy is being held for ransom!"

CHAPTER TWO

S ammy's eyes widened. "When did you find those letters?

David's head tilted and his eyes rolled up as he thought. "Saturday morning. After the buggy was taken."

"Were these letters in any certain order when you picked them up?"

"Can't say," said the Amishman. "They weren't spelled out in a line. That way they weren't. They were like snuggled together."

"Did you get all the letters that were there?"

"I don't know. I think so."

"Do you mind if we take the letters with us? If it is a special message, maybe Brian and I can figure it out."

David shook his head. "Take them." He brushed the letters off the desk into a used, white letter-size envelope. "Already my wife and I pretty much wasted our time."

"Soon," said Brian as the letters spilled into the envelope. "Four of the letters spell *soon.*"

"I saw the word *phone* in the letters," said Sammy. "But there could be hundreds of word possibilities."

"Hum, *phone soon,*" muttered Brian. His mind scurried off in an attempt to create a sentence. Finally he said, "*We will phone soon.* I bet that's what the message says."

"Let's not rush it," said Sammy. "Wait until we have time to look at all the possibilities." His eyes shifted from his friend to the carriage parts lying around the shop floor. He noted the framework of the carriages were identical. "The buggies all look alike," he said. "How will we know the missing buggy if we find it?"

Both teenagers looked at David Fisher for an answer.

"Come here onct just a little," said David, walking over to the fabric rack. He mumbled something in Pennsylvania German when he noticed some wrinkles in the roll of material. He reached and placed his hand on the roll above. "The buggy's gray, but you can tell it by its new upholstery." He ran his hand across the raised pattern. "It's a brown crushed velvet with a double swirl design."

The aspiring detectives moved closer to absorb the details of the cloth and its design. "Wow, I thought the Amish were supposed to be plain," said Brian feeling the fancy material.

"Yah, the Amish are drifting like everyone else," replied David, stating a fact.

"How about the wheels?" asked Sammy. "Anything different about them?"

"Wheels are pretty much the same," said the Amishman, walking over to a wheel leaning against the wall. "But, there is something. Look here onct." He tilted the wheel toward the boys.

The teenager sleuths moved closer, eager to learn from the visual aid.

"Most wheels run on what we call a flat stock metal rim." David ran his fingers across the flat rim from one side to the other. "I'd say three-fourths of the buggies have wheels like these. Now Amos Zook's buggy has half-round steel rims."

"How are they different from the flat stock rims?" asked Brian.

The Amishman moved his hand in an arc across the rim. "Instead of all the flat surface riding on the road, it don't. See, the surface is humped. That way only the raised part of the rim touches the road. There's less friction."

"Why don't all buggies have the curved rims?" asked Brian.

The Amishman raised his eyebrows and smiled. "Because they cost twice as much as the flat-rimmed wheels."

Sammy glanced out the front window for the third time since he arrived at the shop. "So, we're looking for a gray buggy with wheel rims that are slightly curved and brown upholstery that's crushed velvet with a double swirl design," he said mechanically without taking his eyes away from the window. Then he added in a mysterious tone, "Did you know there's a man outside, standing beside a truck? He's been out there for the last fifteen minutes."

David went to the window. "I wasn't expecting—" He took a good look at the truck and then at the man. He was in his late forties, medium height, thin, with graying hair. The Amishman smiled. "It's George Brock. He has a welding shop. You go down here a piece to where the road bends around the bridge. His shop's about a quarter a mile up the road already. He's not so much liked."

"Another suspect," announced Brian, pushing his way to the window.

"Is he a competitor of yours?" added Sammy and wondered why the man remained by his truck.

"His business is different yet," said David, taking another peek. "He just does welding. He works his shop full of wrought iron poles for bird feeders and flower pots. He even has pot racks and railing and such stuff."

"But don't you do welding?" asked Sammy.

David looked away from the window and pointed at one of the carriage bodies. "I build and repair buggies. Welding wheel rims and metal frames I do."

"You don't do any other welding?" asked Sammy.

"Yah, sometimes I do some small iron jobs when business slows." Sammy had heard enough. He added George Brock's name to his list of suspects.

"Do you know why he's out there?" asked Brian.

David shrugged and shook his head.

"Maybe Mr. Brock will come in when we leave," said Brian. "Right, Sammy?"

"Let's find out. Come on, let's go." Sammy looked back at the Amishman. "We'll be on the lookout for your buggy, Mr. Fisher. Thanks for the information. And we'll see if those letters mean anything."

David nodded and watched as the two teenage detectives left the shop and headed for their bikes across the road.

Sammy tried not to show interest in the man as they passed. But the teenager did nod his head and smiled.

George Brock did not smile back. Instead he leaned against the truck. "Hey, you Sammy and Brian?" he yelled.

The boys stopped. How did he know their names?

Sammy backed up and turned. "Yes, I'm Sammy Wilson and this is Brian Helm," he said, pointing to his friend. He waited, wondering what Mr. Brock would have to say next.

But Brock said nothing. He appeared confused and stared at the boys as if deciding whether to continue the conversation. Finally he said, "My name's George Brock. Detective Ben Phillips said you boys could help me."

Sammy looked at the beat-up truck and then at George Brock. "How can we help you?" he asked.

Brock nodded his head. "My place is just across the bridge and up the road to the right. Hop in and we can go there to talk."

Sammy glanced at Brian and sensed they were both thinking the same thing. Would it be safe to get into the truck with this man? Still, Brock had mentioned Detective Ben Phillips' name, their good friend at the police station. "Our bikes are across the road."

Brock shook his thumb. "Put them in the back of the truck."

As Brian laid his bike next to Sammy's, he whispered, "If he tries anything funny, you go for his eyes; I'll punch him in the stomach."

Oh, brother, Sammy thought to himself. However, before he stuffed himself into the cab next to Brian, Sammy made sure Brock saw what he did next. He waved to the window of the carriage shop. David Fisher may not be there, he thought, but at least Brock would think the Amishman knew of their departure in his truck.

The truck rattled out onto the country road, headed for Brock's welding shop. The late morning air was warm, but the chalk-colored sky was a warning of changeable weather.

"I called the police," said Brock, keeping his eyes on the road. "Detective Phillips said he would check into it."

Brian sat up straight. "Are you in trouble?"

"Trouble? Yeah, you could say that."

"What kind of trouble?" asked Sammy.

Brock's truck rambled over the small concrete bridge and fought the right turn. "Somebody wants to kill me."

CHAPTER THREE

"**W**ho wants to kill you?" asked Brian Brock kept his eyes on the road. "I don't know. Yesterday I received a phone call. Whoever it was said I would be killed in my welding shop."

"You didn't recognize the voice?" asked Sammy.

"No. The voice was soft and angry," said George. "It was like a whisper. Could have been a man or woman."

George slowed down as he passed a tourist's car parked along the road. To the right and thirty feet away, a creek ran parallel to the road. The tourist was taking pictures of several young Amish boys fishing, a peaceful scene in contrast to the painful subject discussed in the passing truck.

"Which means," said Sammy, "it might be a voice you'd recognize, since the person found it necessary to disguise it. Do you know any reason why someone would want to kill you in your shop?"

"What do you mean?" asked Brock.

Sammy glanced over Brian's head to observe Brock's reaction to the forthcoming answer. "Usually when a person threatens a life, he or she doesn't say where it will happen. It just sounds odd to be told *where* you will die."

"I work around dangerous welding equipment. Maybe this person wants my death to look like an accident."

"Is that your shop there?" asked Brian, pointing to a large cinder-block building on the left.

"Yeah. Hey, someone just ran around behind the shop!" yelled Brock as he abruptly braked, and his truck skidded to a stop.

The boys quickly opened the truck door. "Brian, take the right side. I'll go left. Hurry!" Sammy ran as fast as his uncoordinated legs could carry him. The land sloped upward as Sammy continued to the back. Finally he saw Brian. Both teenagers were breathing hard as they faced each other at the rear of the building.

"See anybody?" puffed Sammy.

Brian shrugged. "No. You?"

Sammy shook his head and glanced around for possible hiding places. The rear of Brock's property was clear of the junk one might expect to see outside a metal shop. The only visible hiding place was a small cluster of trees in the corn field beyond Brock's property.

"Hey, maybe this was a ploy to get us away from Mr. Brock so someone could kill him," said Brian as he turned and ran back toward the front of the shop.

Sammy took a final look around then headed back to join Brian and George Brock. As he walked down the slight incline, he saw a passing buggy on the road. He couldn't tell from that distance if the metal wheels had curved rims or if it had brown upholstery with a double swirl design. He thought about all the Amish buggies that were out there in Lancaster County. He shook his head. Finding the missing buggy was not going to be easy.

Sammy's concentration shifted as he joined George and Brian. Brian seemed disappointed that he hadn't found George Brock being man-handled by the mysterious culprit who was going to do George in.

"Got away, huh? Too bad," said Brock, waving a piece of paper at the boys. "This note was on the door. Here, read it."

Sammy cringed at the way Brock was handling the paper. Any possible incriminating fingerprints would be gone, replaced by Brock's. Sammy, however, pinched the note by the top corner. Next he glanced at the words printed in bold letters. I WILL KILL YOU RIGHT HERE.

There it was again, thought Sammy. Why was it necessary for someone to kill George Brock here at the welding shop? Why was it necessary to kill him at all? And why advertise it? He passed the note to Brian. "Here, be careful. It might have prints."

Brian read the note and immediately his eyes darted about as if killers were lurking behind every tree.

"Any idea who would want to kill you?" asked Sammy.

"I've been thinking about that," answered Brock. "There is somebody who might." Brock paused, apparently thinking of changing his mind, and said, "Barry Bitner. He worked for me. I fired him last week for stealing."

The two young detectives glanced at each other. They had heard that name before. David Fisher had mentioned the teenager as a suspect in the buggy theft.

"Barry Bitner," repeated Sammy. "What did he steal from you, Mr. Brock?"

"Pieces of iron."

Brian shook his head. "Do you really think he wants to kill you because you caught him stealing?"

"He has a temper. When I told him he was fired, he got real mad. Said he didn't steal the iron. That I had no right to fire him." Brock paused.

"And that's it?" said Sammy.

Brock looked down at the ground. "No. He said he'd be back. That I would pay for firing him."

"Could the person you saw running away just now have been Barry?" asked Sammy.

"Yeah, could have been, but I'm not sure."

"Well, then," said Brian, "we have our man ...ah, boy."

Sammy wasn't ready yet to tag Barry as a potential killer. Also he had the feeling Brock was holding back. "Brian," said Sammy with a touch of disappointment in his voice.

"Yeah, I know," answered Brian. "We don't accuse anyone without proof."

Looking at Brock with his intense blue eyes, Sammy asked, "Are you sure it was Barry who took your iron?"

"Had to be. There was nobody else around at the time. I was out giving a price quote on a job. He probably hid the iron in his car then drove it home after work."

Brock had had no proof or eye witnesses, thought Sammy. He had fired Barry based on his suspicions only.

"I don't know what you boys can do to help me. This is a job for the police," said Brock. "Maybe when I show them the note, they'll track down whoever is doing this."

"Maybe," said Sammy. "But I believe some-one just wants to scare you. Give Brian and me a chance to talk this over, and we'll contact you to-morrow morning. Will you be here at your shop?"

"Yes, I expect to be here—dead or alive," Brock said in a morbid tone.

Sammy was beginning to feel sorry for the welder. He glanced up at Brock's homemade sign: George Brock Welding, Wrought Iron Crafts. He then thought of something his father had mentioned the previous day. "My parents are moving their business across the street to the Bird-in-Hand Junction. They're going to need more quilt racks. Could you make the metal arms that hold the quilts?"

George's solemn face suddenly became animated. "Yeah, I know just what you're asking for. I made some for a fellow over on Route 30. How many arms do they want?"

"I'm not sure. You'll have to talk to my parents."

Suddenly Brock smiled. "Bird-in-Hand is only fifteen minutes away. Why don't I drive you home, get the information from your parents, and give them an estimate?"

Sammy was surprised. It was the first time he had seen the man smile. Plus, Brock seemed more interested in acquiring a new customer than in preserving his own life.

Sammy glanced at Brian who was still pinching the threatening note by its corner. "Here, Brian, let me have that," said Sammy as he pulled a tissue from his pocket and carefully wrapped the note. We have to get this evidence to Detective Phillips so it can be checked for fingerprints."

"Why don't I just drop it off after I'm finished at your parents' store?"

"That's a good idea," said Sammy. "The police will need your prints anyway to eliminate them from other prints they might find on the note."

The Bird-in-Hand Country Store was housed in a small frame building next to the post office on Main Street in the village of Bird-in-Hand. The Wilsons lived in an apartment above the store. However, the business had outgrown the potential of the small building, so the Wilsons decided to relocate across the street. Al and Kathy Witmer, owners of the Bird-in-Hand Junction, had a large room available that was much larger than the shop the Wilsons now occupied.

When the young detectives and the welder entered the store, Mrs. Wilson was busy in the main quilt room. Mr. Wilson was placing Amish wall hangings into large plastic bags. Boxes and bags, filled with merchandise, lined the side wall, waiting to be transferred to their new location across the street.

"Dad, this is George Brock," said Sammy. "He has a welding shop over in Lime Valley. He's interested in making the additional metal arms we need to display the quilts."

"Great. Follow me," said Mr. Wilson as he led the way to the small room next to the quilt room. This room, which contained wall hangings and pillow covers, also had a small quilt rack. He gently lifted a quilt from a metal arm so Brock could examine the triangular metal support. "In our new location across the street, we're going to build three nine-foot racks. We'll need about one hundred more metal arms like these. Same size. So if you want to give us your price, we'll consider you for the job."

Sammy and Brian watched through the open doorway as Brock went about the task of taking measurements and making sketches. They both had the same thought, Why would someone want to kill this man?

The thought vanished when a woman entered the shop. Except for the drawn face and worried expression, she was quite attractive. Even though she wore a T-shirt and jeans, she appeared ready for any occasion. She was in her late thirties, had short brown hair with blond highlights, and brown eyes. Because of her slim shape and well-toned arms and legs, Sammy assumed she routinely exercised to stay in shape.

Ms. "Slim-and-Fit" glanced at the signs displayed on the far wall. She frowned and shook her head.

"Something wrong?" asked Sammy.

"Some of those signs are crooked," she said casually as her eyes scanned the room. "Where are the quilts?"

Sammy turned and pointed. "There in the quilt room." He brushed some strands of hair from his face to get a better look at the woman.

Mrs. Wilson walked past them, carrying a quilt, followed by a smiling customer. They headed for the checkout counter.

Ms. "Slim-and-Fit" eyed the quilt Sammy's mother was carrying. "Too pale," she said to herself and turned and entered the quilt room.

Sammy followed, intrigued by the woman's attitude.

She fanned through the quilts displayed on the rack. Then she spotted the bed covered with multiple quilts. The sign on top informed the customers to ask for assistance in folding back the quilts for examination. She looked around at Sammy. "I guess I have to wait for you to flip each quilt so I can get a look at them," she snapped.

The young detective nodded and wondered, What is this woman's problem? Sammy loved to solve problems and Ms. "Slim-and-Fit" certainly had one.

"Do you ever have these quilts on sale?" she asked as Sammy pulled the quilts back, one at a time.

"No, we don't. The quilts are here on consignment. Which means they are still owned by the Amish who made them." Sammy raised the tag from the bottom of the quilt and held it for the customer to see. "This quilt took five hundred hours to make and the price is four hundred ninety-five dollars. The Amish woman who made this quilt gets less than a dollar an hour."

"I know what the word consignment means. And I doubt it took five hundred hours to make this quilt."

Have you ever tried making a quilt? Sammy wanted to say but didn't. Instead, he ignored the statement and added, "Plus, she had the cost of the materials."

The woman said nothing as the teenager continued to pull back each quilt to expose the one beneath it. Finally she said, "That's the one." An unexpected smile materialized. "I like it."

The quilt was the Sunshine and Shadow design, a traditional Amish pattern, made up of black, purple, green, red, and blue cloth squares.

She looked at Sammy as if for the first time. She said apologetically, "I don't mean to be rude, but I'm under a lot of pressure right now. I'm opening my own restaurant." Her eyes returned to the quilt. "I want the quilt to use as a wall hanging in the restaurant."

Before Sammy could comment, Mr. Brock leaned in from the side room. "Ah, Alex Austin, I thought I recognized your voice. I didn't expect to see you here."

At the sound of Brock's voice, Alex Austin whipped around to face the person interrupting her purchase. "Oh, it's you, George. I'm thinking of buying a quilt for the restaurant. What are you doing here?"

"I'm giving the Wilsons a price quote on quilt brackets. Did you know they're moving their business across the street?"

Alex shook her head.

"Well, good luck with the quilt. I gotta run. See you later." Saying that, George hurried to the checkout counter and interrupted Mr. Wilson. "I got the measurements. I'll see you get my price for a hundred metal arms." He brushed past Brian, left the store, and hurried to his truck.

Alex was noticeably surprised at Brock's quick departure. She even moved to the room's doorway to make sure he had left the shop. She turned and pointed at the Sunshine and Shadow pattern. "I'll take that quilt."

The teenager called his mother, and together they slid the chosen quilt from between the others on the bed. Mrs. Wilson then escorted Alex Austin to the counter to complete the sale.

Brian Helm was all excited as he joined his partner in the small quilt room. "Did I hear the name Alex Austin?" he whispered.

"So you heard," said Sammy quietly. He whipped out his note pad and opened it to the page labeled SUSPECTS. "Yeah, it's strange how the names on the missing-buggy list are coming up in connection with George Brock. Barry Bitner and now Alex Austin." He placed a heavy check mark after each of the two names.

"Hey," said Brian, "maybe if we check out her restaurant, we'll find the stolen buggy."

"Good idea," said Sammy. "Let's see if she left the store yet."

As the two boys entered the main room, Alex was lugging her purchase out the door and across the porch. They moved toward the closed door and watched as she placed the plastic-wrapped quilt on the back seat of her car. But before the boys had a chance to get to their bikes, she had pulled out and headed west on Main Street. Her car quickly blended in with the flow of tourist traffic.

Sammy slipped behind the counter and quietly asked his mother if Alex Austin had mentioned the location of her restaurant. She had not. Even the address on the approved personal check was her home address. He quickly wrote Alex's home address in his notebook.

"I know who can tell us where the restaurant is," said Brian.

Sammy also knew possible steps to explore to learn the new restaurant's location. But he would hear his friend out. "Who can tell us?" he asked.

"Brenda up at the Snack Counter," said Brian. "She knows everything that goes on around this area."

"I was thinking of Anne at the Little Book Shop," added Sammy.

"Yeah, well, Brenda knows more. And besides, you can't eat books for lunch," said Brian. "And I'm hungry for a hot dog and sauerkraut."

Sammy glanced at his watch. "Your stomach is right on schedule. Should we take our bikes or walk up?"

"Let's rough it," said Brian as though he was getting ready for a three-mile hike instead of a one-block stroll.

Brenda's Snack Counter was part of The Farmer's Market, a favorite stopping place for tourists. The market sold meat products, baked goods, crafts, and much more. Even though the seating at the snack bar consisted only of tall stools at the counter, quite rustic by modern standards, the food was great. Best of all, for Sammy and Brian, the price was right.

Bird-in-Hand's two young sleuths grabbed two stools when they became available and ordered hot dogs with sauerkraut on the side.

"So what are you crime fighters up to now?" asked Brenda as she placed their order in front of them. She was a platinum blond, petite, and in her forties.

Sammy leaned in close and whispered, "Do you know an Alex Austin?"

"Sure," she said, leaning her head to the west. "She's opening a restaurant in Smoketown."

Brian tipped his stool toward Sammy and said, "See, I told you she would know." But the stool tilted too far and started to fall. Brian's legs were tangled in the rungs of the stool. He quickly grabbed the edge of the counter as the stool slowly slid to the floor. His legs were trapped. But he hung on and pulled himself up, straining, allowing his head to bob up above the counter top. His nose hovered over his hot dog and the small plate of sauerkraut. "Ugh, ah," he managed to sputter as his face looked into Brenda's. "I'm...I'm okay, Brenda," he labored, "I just like to do chin-ups before I eat." This time Brian didn't bother to smile.

Sammy quickly untangled Brian's legs and slid the stool away, allowing Brian's feet to touch the floor. "Hey, are you okay?"

Brian slithered to a standing position. "Yeah, I'm fine," he said, still feeling wobbly. "Wow, Brenda, you need another sign up there on the wall."

"Really?" responded Brenda with a snicker.

"Yeah. One that says, 'Counter stools can be dangerous to your health.' "

Brenda smiled and watched Brian reseat himself in front of his food. "I was thinking about a sign that says, 'Brian can be dangerous to Brenda's Snack Counter.' "

Brian sheepishly cast his eyes downward and took a bite of his hot dog and a fork full of sauerkraut.

Glancing at Sammy, Brenda asked, "Are you boys working on a big case? Is Alex Austin involved?"

Sammy, not willing to reveal information about an on-going case, replied, "To tell you the truth, we're not sure what we're working on." Which wasn't really a lie. However, Sammy had an uneasy feeling that more trouble lay ahead.

Brenda wanted to hear more, but she had other customers to serve. "Well, if you need help, let me know," she said, leaving the young detectives to finish their lunch.

After lunch, the boys walked across the parking lot and entered The Little Book Shop. Sammy found that most detective work consisted of gathering information. On their last case, *Jonathan's Journal*, the boys had gotten valuable information through their research on local history in books at the Historical Society. This time, Sammy had a hunch that people would supply the information needed. And Anne, who ran the book shop, would be one of those people.

Anne looked up from a pile of used books she had just assembled on the counter. "Hi, Sammy, Brian. Nice day for sleuthing," she said as she pushed the books aside. Anne was around forty; she had short-cropped brown hair and blue eyes.

Brian stood tall and in his best melodramatic voice said, "Anne, we fight crime wherever we find it—in any kind of weather." He raised his arms as though to shield his face. "In rain, sleet, and snow, we face—"

"You sound like a mail carrier," interrupted Anne.

"Well, we do deliver," said Brian as a big smile swept across his face.

"Anne," said Sammy, anxious to get on with the investigation, "do you know why someone would steal an Amish buggy?"

Anne stared at the teenager with a blank expression, then smiled. "I have to think about that. Oh, are you referring to the buggy taken from David Fisher's Carriage Shop?"

Brian was surprised that Anne knew of the missing buggy. "Yeah, dumb, huh?" he said, eager to get Anne on his side.

"Stealing anything is dumb," said Anne. "You may get rid of what you stole, but the guilt of having stolen it stays with you for the rest of your life."

While Brian was digesting Anne's "dumbness" theory, Sammy peeled back several notebook pages. "Anne, do you know Wally Mills?"

In reaction to the question, Anne's arm jerked, spilling the books over the counter. She grinned. "That's why I don't own a china shop."

Anne's mother came out from the back office. Joanne was seventy-two and had what she called gray, "stroobly" hair. She was always there to help her daughter in the shop. "You're asking about Wally Mills, the antique dealer in Ronks?"

Sammy nodded his head. "That's the one."

"Why are you asking?" asked Anne. "Do you think he stole the buggy?"

"He's one of several names we're checking on," said Sammy, helping Anne and her mother to restack the books.

"He's one of my best customers. Loves to read." She paused, then added, "Wally doesn't need any more trouble in his life."

"He's in trouble?" asked Brian, suspecting Mr. Mills might have a criminal record.

"No, not really trouble. It's just Wally isn't the same since his wife was killed two years ago."

"Oh? How was she killed?" asked Sammy.

"A truck ran a stop sign and hit her car. She died later at the hospital."

"That's rough," said Sammy. "Do you know who was driving the truck?"

"Yeah, George Brock."

CHAPTER FOUR

T he two teenage detectives looked at each other in astonishment.

"George Brock, the welder?" asked Brian. "The one over in Lime Valley?"

"Yep, the same," said Anne, walking her books over to an empty shelf. She carefully placed each book side by side with the spine showing.

Sammy moved aside to allow a customer to place books on the counter. "Hey, you're busy," he said. "We'll check with you later." He pulled Brian's arm and moved away as other customers formed a line. "And, Anne, if you come up with anything on the buggy, let us know."

"Yeah, I'll do that," returned Anne.

"So George Brock killed Wally's wife," said Brian as he squirmed into a comfortable position, lying across the bottom of Sammy's bed. The two teenagers were in Sammy's bedroom above the shop. This was where they did their brainstorming. Sammy usually sat at his oak desk facing his partner. They would ask each other questions, throw ideas around, and hopefully come up with answers that would further their investigation.

Brian's feet dangled over the side of the bed as his eyes concentrated on the ceiling above. "If I was George Brock and my life was threatened, Wally Mills would be the first person I'd name as a suspect. Why didn't he?"

Sammy sat back in his chair and thought for a moment. He then interlocked his fingers behind his head and looked up at the ceiling, joining Brian's area of concentration. "If Wally Mills wanted to kill Brock, he would have done it two years ago when his wife was killed. That's when his anger was probably the strongest." Sammy glanced over at the psychology books that lined part of his wall-to-wall book shelf. "Also George is probably trying to forget the incident. With guilt like that, the mind tries to blot out the memory."

"Maybe it took Wally two years to plan the perfect murder," said Brian. "And now he's ready."

Sammy shook his head. "So now, two years later, he warns Brock that he's going to kill him in his welding shop? What's perfect about that?"

"Well, a warning like that would scare me," said Brian. "Maybe Wally wants Brock to suffer like he's been suffering these two years. Right, Sammy?"

"I can't think of a better idea, Brian," said Sammy, wanting to improve Brian's self-esteem.

Brian grinned and nodded.

"But," said Sammy, "Brock didn't seem frightened. Remember, he was all business when I mentioned the making of the quilt racks."

"So Wally's scheme isn't working," added Brian. "Brock isn't scared."

Sammy released his fingers from their grip behind his head and stood. "Maybe Brock wants to die. He might think he deserves to die for killing Wally's wife."

Brian propped himself up with his left elbow, looked at his companion, and said excitedly, "And that's why his welding business is suffering. He just doesn't care anymore."

"Let's not get hung up on Wally Mills. We can't eliminate Barry Bitner as a suspect," said Sammy, standing and moving to the window. "And who knows? If we keep poking, we might come up with others who want Brock dead."

Brian lifted himself from the bed. "What about the missing buggy?" asked Brian.

Sammy watched as an Amish horse and buggy slowly led a string of cars past the shop. The image was that of a passing parade with tourists lining both sides of the street. The motorists were not pleased, but the strolling tourists were. It gave them a chance to see an Amish buggy up close and an opportunity to dash across the street between cars.

The teenager glanced to his left. The thought of his parents moving their business down, across the street, made him sad. He was going to miss this room and this vantage point he had of Main Street.

"Well," repeated Brian, "what about the missing buggy?"

Sammy stepped back from the window and turned toward the desk. He reached into his pocket and carefully slid out the envelope containing the cut-out letters. He lifted the flap and spilled the contents onto the desk. He shook the envelope and glanced inside, making sure all pieces fell out. Next he spread and turned some pieces so they were right side up. Then he counted them. "Twenty," he finally said with a look of anticipation.

y w d R O
l e n s y i
o h i P o u
i u l

"You think the letters are going to tell us who took the buggy?" asked Brian.

Sammy studied the letters. He allowed time for his mind to register the letters and look for patterns. He knew the subconscious mind liked dealing with word puzzles. It was like the dreams he had at night, where the subconscious took parts of his life and scrambled the pieces. When the pieces were put together correctly, he had a message, a message from his subconscious. Well, thought Sammy, if the mind can take a message and break it into pieces, it certainly can take pieces and recreate the message.

The teenager smiled to himself as his blue eyes squinted and roamed through the mixture of letters. Meaningless now, but in the right order... He allowed his fingers, on their own, to automatically push several letters into position. Y-E-L-L-O-W.

Brian shook his head. "Those letters are not going to tell us who took the buggy."

"Well, at least it will be fun seeing what words we can make from them. And the words just might reveal a message."

"Yeah, I can see it now," said Brian with a comic flair. "I HAVE A YELLOW PENCIL BOX."

"Sorry, but some of those letters aren't here," said Sammy putting an end to Brian's funny response. Then he shifted the mood. "I'm going to work with these letters for awhile. Suppose you check on Barry Bitner and Alex Austin. Snoop around and ask questions. Check their homes and Alex's restaurant. Maybe you'll get lucky and find the buggy."

"Right, chief," said Brian, saluting. "I'll report back here at headquarters tonight at seven." He snapped his head to punctuate his statement. "And what are you going to do?"

Sammy clapped his hands together as if killing a fly. "I think I just developed an interest in antiques."

Gray clouds sneaked back again and covered the brief, late afternoon sun. Several drops of rain were an introduction to the drizzle that was sure to follow. Sammy hustled his bike under a tree and glanced at the sign on the front lawn. The brick house itself was ancient. The many old objects on display across the porch confirmed the sign's simple message: Wally Mills, Antiques.

The paper sign on the door read, Ring the bell for service. Sammy did.

The man who presented himself at the opened door was exactly what the teenage detective had expected. Wally Mills looked to be in his fifties but was probably younger. The death of his wife had drained the gentleness and enthusiasm from his frail body. His voice was rough, impersonal, and all business.

"What are you looking for today?" he announced. "If I don't have it, I can get it for you."

When Wally opened the door wider to step out onto the porch, Sammy could see back through the house and out the back kitchen window. What he saw looked very much like a gray Amish buggy. His heart raced as he thought of what to say.

"What is it you're looking for?"

The teenager thought he would get right to it. "Do you have any Amish buggies for sale?"

"No. No, I don't. Not at the moment. But I can get one for you."

"I'm looking for a buggy that has curved rims and brown upholstery with a double swirl pattern."

A strange look came over Wally's face. "You're not here to buy anything are you?"

"No, I'm...Sammy Wilson."

"I know who you are. You and your friend think you're detectives. You go around asking a lot of questions. Well, what do you want to know?"

Sammy thought he also would use the direct business-like approach. "George Brock is receiving threats on his life. Your name came up as a possible suspect."

Wally was quiet, listening to the raindrops that accented Sammy's words. Words that brought back a two-year-old memory. *The crash...The phone call...The hospital...The grave.*

Finally he said, "Because he killed my wife. That's why you suspect me. Well, let me tell you. Killing him will not bring my wife back. We both have to live with what happened. No, I'm not the person you want. Go find someone else who wants Brock dead." He turned away from Sammy, went to the end of the porch, and looked toward the back of the house.

"Thank you, Mr. Mills. I'm sorry, but I have to check these things out," said Sammy to Wally's back.

"Jack, Jack!" yelled Wally. "You finished unloading?"

"Yeah, he's coming out," said a voice, followed by the sound of a horse and buggy rolling forward on the paved driveway.

Wally waved as the Amishman brought his horse and buggy to the front and out onto the wet road. The antique dealer then turned to Sammy. "That's Aaron Glick. He just delivered an antique blanket chest."

"Hey, Dad, I put the chest in the garage," said a man in his early twenties, stepping up onto the porch to escape the rain. Water beaded on the baseball cap that covered most of his blond hair. His brightly colored T-shirt was wet and stuck to his skin. He took off his glasses and wiped them with a tissue. "I hate it when rain gets on my glasses."

The young man standing before Sammy was not a stranger. He knew Jack from seeing

him at local auctions. What he didn't know was
that this man he knew as Jack was Wally Mills'
son.

"Hi, Jack," said Sammy as the man fitted
his dry glasses back over his ears.

"Hey, Sammy," said Jack, after he focused
on the teenager standing behind his father. "You
missed a good sale last week at the Conestoga
Auction. They had a couple of old baseball cards."

"Yeah, I heard," returned Sammy. "I was
busy."

"You and Brian still tracking down criminals?"

Before Sammy could answer, Wally pointed
his thumb at the teenager. "He thinks I might be
one. George Brock believes someone is out to kill
him. Your friend here suspects I'm the culprit."
He reached into a pocket and pulled out a lollipop. "You see, I'm a sweet guy." He undid the
paper and stuck the lollipop into his mouth.

"My father's trying to give up smoking,"
replied Jack.

Wally pulled the candy from his mouth. He
smiled cunningly. "I'd rather make several visits
to my dentist than one visit to my grave."

Jack put his arm around his father.
"Sammy, my father might have a reason for wanting Brock dead, but he wouldn't do it. Two years
ago Brock's wife left him. He had a hard time
adjusting. My mother happened to be at the wrong
place at the wrong time. Brock did a bad thing

when he killed my mother with his truck, but that doesn't make him a bad person. Look, Sammy, we all suffered. But now it's behind us. Life goes on."

Sammy felt that something was wrong. Jack's words didn't quite match the look in his eyes. But something did match. The bright colored T-shirt Jack was wearing matched the color of the shirts he usually wore at the auctions—*yellow*.

CHAPTER FIVE

B rian flopped down on the bed. It was five minutes to seven, and Sammy was already busy at the computer. Brian made a face. "You know, I'm going to miss this room when you move across the street."

Sammy shrugged. "We'll have plenty of room. The bedroom's going to be a little smaller, but we can use the room next to it as our research room." He continued to concentrate on the monitor.

"But we're going to use your new bedroom for our brainstorming. Right, Sammy?"

"Brian, you're not going to lose your comfortable spot on the bed."

A large smile swept across Brian's face. "Hey, and if you put your computer in the research room, you'll have room for a television set on your desk."

The large oak chair scuffed sideways across the wooden floor. Sammy's face now bypassed the monitor. A pair of soft, understanding blue eyes locked onto Brian's hazel eyes. A slow and gentle voice said, "Brian, do you know why I don't watch a lot of television?" Each word was meant to rivet Brian's attention on the answer.

"No, but you're going to tell me. Right, Sammy?"

The teenager said, "When we watch television, we're watching other people earn a living, while our time is slipping away. I would rather spend my time reading and having experiences that prepare me for *my* future, not someone else's."

Brian watched as the chair and its occupant slid back behind the computer. "Yeah, me, too," he said. He interlocked his fingers behind his head and slowly leaned back on the bed. His eyes fixed on the ceiling, but his mind was thinking of the opportunities that lay beyond.

Sammy stopped typing, looked up at the ceiling, and searched for something moving. There was nothing. He smiled. "We'll do the brainstorming in the bedroom, but we're not taking your spider friend, Larry, along."

Brian smiled. He really didn't like spiders. But he was always ready with a story about Larry. "That's the problem with moving, you have to give up old friends. I'll miss old Larry." He gave a dramatic sigh. "But, I'm willing to make the sacrifice. It won't be too bad though. Larry told me his grandfather has a split-level web over in your new bedroom. Said I should look him up when we get over there."

"A split-level, huh? Larry's grandfather must be rich."

"Well, yeah. There's a lot of money in silk," said Brian, his face grinning.

Sammy made a sour face, pushed the delete button on the keyboard, and continued typing.

The silence that followed made Sammy uncomfortable. He knew that his partner was waiting for him to finish at the computer before reporting what he found out about Barry Bitner. He decided to encourage Brian to continue with his lighthearted humor. "I haven't seen Larry around on the ceiling for a couple of days. Is he still working as an undercover cop?"

Brian, whose thoughts had drifted, replied, "What...? What undercover cop?"

"The last time you talked about your spider friend, he was working as an undercover police officer."

"No, he gave up that job. He said he wanted to earn more money."

Sammy shook his head, took a deep breath, and said, "So what's Larry into now?"

Brian needed only a second to think, then he said, "He's selling shoes."

"I can't see how he can make a lot of money selling shoes."

"Hey, think about it. Spiders have eight

legs. They have to buy four pair of shoes at a time."

Sammy smiled then stopped typing. He hadn't stopped because of Brian's commentary—it was important to compile and record the events of the day while they were still fresh in his mind. He had finished his work and now the computer would have the responsibility of recalling the facts when they were needed.

The aspiring detective closed his eyes and went limp in the chair. He was tired and needed a break. After a few seconds he stood, walked to the front window, and glanced across the street and to his left. Finally he said, "The house we're moving to is supposed to be one of the oldest houses in Bird-in-Hand. Dates back to the early 1700's, before the village of Bird-in-Hand even existed." He smiled. "Maybe Larry's grandfather can tell us about secret treasures hidden in the walls."

"Hey, I never thought of that," said Brian, jumping from the bed, leaving his images of his spider friend behind. "Yeah, who knows what's hidden in the walls and buried in the basement after all these years."

Now that his buddy had returned to a serious frame of mind, Sammy turned from the window and said, "Let's save that for another day. What did you find out about Barry Bitner?"

Brian pulled his worn notebook from his back pocket. He flipped through several pages then stopped. "I went over to Lime Valley and talked with a neighbor of Barry's. According to her, Barry is eighteen and lives at home with his parents. Graduated from high school last year. Oh, and you know the wood that Barry was supposed to have stolen from Mike Herr? According to the neighbor, Barry thought the wood was junk because it was piled beside the road."

"It's possible, I guess," said Sammy as he returned to his chair. He tapped again on the computer's keyboard. "Anything else on Barry?"

"Yeah, Barry has a temper. Gets into a lot of fights. The neighbor said that Barry thinks people are always picking on him." Brian went around the desk, leaned over Sammy's shoulder, and glanced at the monitor. He nodded his head in approval. He retraced his steps to again face his audience of one. "And she's never seen Barry with iron bars *or* an Amish buggy."

Sammy stopped typing, waited, and then looked at his friend. "That's it?"

"That's it," repeated Brian, closing his notebook and returning it to his pocket. "I'll check on Alex Austin tomorrow. Now," said Brian moving closer to the desk and pointing to the white envelope, "any luck with the letters?"

"I made some new words. But the hardest part is to have the words form a sentence without having any letters left over."

"But you can do it. Right, Sammy?"

There was no denying it. Sammy was anxious to unscramble the letters and reveal their true meaning. Even if the message wasn't related to the missing buggy, Sammy's mind craved the challenge and the creative exercise. "Let's give it another shot," he said, dumping the envelope's contents onto the desk top.

The letters were definitely taken from one or more magazines. He arranged the pieces so they were right-side-up and in the upright position. For example, what looked like p's might in fact be d's and, likewise, what looked like u's could be n's.

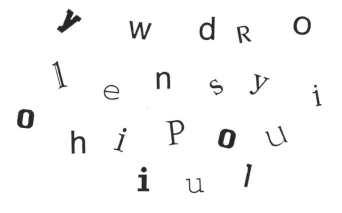

Now that the letters were ready, the boys started to manipulate them. They formed words like *sour, whip, yield,* and *only.*

"We need to form words that will work together to form a sentence," said Sammy. "Here let me try first, then you can try."

Brian frowned and stepped back.

Phone soon were the words that Sammy remembered from the carriage shop. He took the letters for *phone* but found no other *n* for the word *soon*. But he did see the word *will* and with another *i*, he placed them before *phone*. "*I will phone*," said Sammy.

"*You*," shouted Brian. "*I will phone you.*"

Sammy counted the remaining letters. "We still have seven more letters to go," he said. Switching them around into different positions, he finally settled on the words, *your* and *sid*. He looked up at Brian and said, "*Sid* could be short for *Sidney. I will phone you, your sid.* What do you think, Brian?" asked Sammy as he entered that possibility into the computer.

"But the Amish don't have phones," said Brian. He reached over and broke up the words *your sid.*

"Some of the Amish do," said Sammy. "The ones who have businesses sometimes have a telephone at the edge of their property. That way they can order supplies or talk business. But they won't have a phone in their house. It encourages social chatting."

Brian took his eyes from the letters, smiled, and gazed at the pair of serious blue eyes. "You mean they have a phone sitting on the grass next to the road?" he asked, knowing this was not the case.

"No, the phone's kept in a shed, usually near the end of the lane. I'm going to check with David Fisher. See if he has one some-where."

"Hey, look here." Brian had rearranged the seven letters to form the words *so* and *rudy*. "It now becomes, *so I will phone you, rudy*."

Sammy shook his head. "But there's an *i* left over."

"Maybe there was an extra *i*."

"I don't think so," said Sammy, "but I'll put it in the computer anyway."

The boys continued, making new words. Two words caught Sammy's attention, *soon* and *die*. He thought of two other words that would make sense and the letters were there. He slid the words around to make, *you will die soon*.

Brian frowned. "There are six letters yet to use."

Sammy looked at the letters, allowing his subconscious mind to do the work. His hand reached out for the *u* and *r* and placed them after the other words. The remaining four letters he grouped together to finish the message.

The teenage detectives read the words, *you will die soon u r hipy*.

"Hey, it makes sense," said Brian. "The Amish could look like hippies to some people. But there's a p missing in the word hippie."

Sammy punched away at the keyboard. "Maybe he got tired cutting out letters and did it the easy way." He stopped typing and glanced up. "Look, this is crazy. Too many possibilities exist here." He pushed his chair away from the desk and stood. "If you're really going to kill somebody, why not just do it? Why fool around with telephone calls, notes at doors, and cut-out letters?"

Brian spun around and faced the bed. He raised his hands over his head. "So no one's really going to be killed. Right, Sammy?"

"I doubt it," said Sammy to Brian's back.

Brian collapsed, face first, onto the bed. He lay still, his face smothered in the blanket.

"You all right, Brian?" asked Sammy

His buddy rolled over onto his back and stared at the ceiling. "I was wrong."

Sammy was relieved when Brian spoke. "You were wrong about what?"

"I was wrong when I said this was a dumb case. This case isn't dumb; it's confusing."

Sammy went to the window and peered at the thinning traffic on Main Street. "You're right, Brian, this case is confusing, but there's order in it somewhere. Because somehow, the missing buggy, the threat on George Brock's life, and maybe these scrambled letters are all tied together. There's something here we're overlooking."

Suddenly, there was a knock at the door.

"Sammy," said Mrs. Wilson, "you're wanted on the phone."

"Be right back," said Sammy as he hurried past his friend.

When the door closed, Brian moaned and slipped his hands behind his head. Order? How can there be order in this case? he wondered. What he would like to order was a hot dog and sauerkraut. Boy, was he hungry. He wished Sammy would hurry back.

Brian's eyes scurried across the ceiling and searched the four corners of the room. No spiders in sight. He glanced at the far wall. Larry wasn't there. Maybe the spider had already climbed down the wall, thought Brian. Maybe he's sneaking across the floor. Maybe he's under the bed. Maybe he's crawling up the bed and over the blanket toward me. Maybe he's creeping up my... Brian screamed and jumped from the bed, his hands striking out. He looked down, searching his clothing, looking for any black spots that moved.

Sammy rushed into the room. "Brian, what's wrong?"

To escape embarrassment, Brian skidded into his fun mode. "Larry told me you were coming, so I stood to give you the respect you deserve."

"Did he also tell you to scream?"

"No, *sir*, that was my own original idea, *sir*," said Brian, standing at attention and saluting.

Sammy figured Brian had fallen asleep on the bed and had a nightmare. But the phone call he had just received from George Brock was its own nightmare. Someone was in the clump of trees behind Brock's property. And that person had a rifle.

CHAPTER SIX

"**B**rian, that was George Brock. He's not sure, but he thinks there is somebody hiding in the trees behind the shop. And the person might be holding a rifle." Sammy's comment and serious blue eyes quickly put a chill over Brian's intended humor.

"Where's Brock now?" asked Brian.

"He's still at his shop," replied Sammy. "He said he was looking out of his back window and saw somebody among the trees. It's pretty far away, but the person was carrying something. Brock thinks it could be a rifle. He wants us to come over to investigate."

"Just us? We're going to confront someone who maybe has a rifle?"

"No, I already called our friend, Detective Phillips, at home. He said he'd be right over and give us a ride to Lime Valley."

"And of course, since he'll be there," said Brian, "he just might want to walk with us to the trees. Right, Sammy?"

"That's exactly what I had in mind," said the young detective. "If I know Ben, he'll insist on it."

Fifteen minutes later Detective Ben Phillips and the boys approached the welding shop from the east end. The sun was taking its last look at the countryside, and the creek to the left was coasting toward the dam on the other side of the concrete bridge. Phillips parked the car off the road to the right.

Sammy pointed out the trees at the edge of the field behind Brock's property. And as Sammy predicted, Phillips insisted on leading the way to investigate. They closed the car doors silently and made a wide circle to the back.

Before them, rows upon rows of corn provided evidence of the richness of Lancaster County soil. Then came the cluster of twelve to fifteen trees. These trees that provided shade and rest for the weary farmer, now provided potential danger for the newcomers.

Brian was the last to enter the kingdom of the trees. He felt the coolness and the fear of the mysterious branches. The slowly creeping shadows stimulated his vivid imagination and put menacing obstacles in his way. The low hanging branches that grabbed at his arms could also hide hideous creatures. He swallowed hard. Running up against a monster carrying a gun could shorten the life of any enthusiastic explorer. With his heart pounding, Brian moved in close behind Sammy and Phillips.

They hadn't gone far past the first couple of trees when Phillip's outspread hands caused the boys to stop. He turned his head and whispered, "Stay here. I see someone."

Sammy sidestepped behind a tree because of possible gunfire. Brian scurried behind Sammy because that's where he wanted to be.

Detective Ben Phillips slid his gun from beneath his coat. He moved cautiously toward the dark shape. The menacing figure was twenty feet away and had its back to Phillips. The dark form was that of a young man. He was clutching something in his right hand. The individual was so engrossed in watching the welding shop, that Phillips had no trouble in sneaking up close behind him.

The detective quickly grabbed and shook the individual's right arm, causing a metal object to fall to the ground. "I'm a police officer," he said and swung the person around and pushed him against a tree.

The scared, tense figure shrieked and squirmed. Anybody, facing a six-foot-two, two-hundred-twenty-pound detective holding a gun, had something to yell about.

Tonight, Detective Ben Phillips was dressed casually. But there was nothing casual about the man himself. His mysterious thin mustache seemed to compensate for his receding hairline. More threatening was Phillips' dark penetrating eyes, which alone could compel a crook to run to a jail cell and lock himself in. Since Phillips had the person pinned, the tree would be his holding cell for the moment.

But the individual against the tree was not a man. He was a frightened teenager about eighteen years old. His dark clothes and black curly hair blended in with the trees. His round face showed the guilt and pain of failure.

Phillips released his grip on the boy. "What are you doing here?" he asked, his eyes set and waiting for an answer.

"Look, I'm Barry Bitner, and—"

"You're the one who stole the iron from Mr. Brock," interrupted Brian.

"No, that's why I'm here," said Barry, still shaking. "I—I know this sounds strange, but I was just driving by and saw movement through the window of Mr. Brock's welding shop."

"So you thought you'd just drop in and kill George Brock with this gun," said Brian. He bent over and snatched up the long metal object expecting it to be a rifle. Instead, he was holding a tire iron. Brian shrugged. "Okay, so you were going to hit him over the head with this tire iron."

"I brought that tire iron from the car for my own protection." Barry leaned back against the tree and took a deep breath. "I have no reason to kill Brock."

Detective Ben Phillips put his gun away and restated his question, "What are you doing here?"

Barry hesitated then said, "Brock accused me of stealing some iron. But I didn't do it. That means somebody else did. So when I saw some movement in the shop, I figured somebody might be stealing more iron. If I caught the thief, I could prove I didn't do it."

Sammy took a step forward. "Didn't it occur to you that it was Mr. Brock in the building?"

"That's just it. Brock never works at night. Look, when I worked for him, he told me he did volunteer work at the hospital in the evenings. And his truck isn't here. What else was I to think?"

"Maybe, said Brian, "you could think that Mr. Brock just lives up the road here. He can walk to the shop, leaving his truck at home."

"I hate to break bad news to you," said Sammy, pointing to the building, "but George Brock is down there. He called us. That's why we're here."

"Okay, but I didn't know that. Hey, I was getting ready to sneak down to look in the back window when you came."

Phillips took a long look at Barry, reached over, and relieved Brian of the tire iron. "Here," he said, "put this back in your car and go. But if anything ever happens to George Brock, you're the person I'll come to first. You understand?"

Barry's strained look now changed to anger. He glared at the teenage detectives. His look was so intense that Brian raised his arms in self-defense, thinking Barry was ready to swing the tire iron. But instead, Barry turned abruptly, squeezing the bar in his fist. "I didn't do anything wrong," he snarled and stomped away into the clearing.

"That temper will get him into trouble some-day," said Phillips. He pointed to the back door of the shop. "I think you better go tell Brock it was a false alarm. I'll wait for you in the car." The de-tective, with his hands in his pockets, ambled off to the road. This encounter had been only a trivial annoyance for the detective. Most of his confron-tations were a lot worse.

Brian realized that he and his buddy were now alone. He snapped his head around and glanced in various directions. He tugged at Sammy's arm. "C-c-come on, let's go. It's getting dark."

Blue pierced through Sammy's squinting eyes and focused on Barry's distant form, becom-ing smaller and smaller. "There's something else we should be afraid of, Brian."

"W-w-what's that?"

"I think we just stirred up a hornet's nest."

CHAPTER SEVEN

I t had been a long day for Sammy and especially weird. As he crawled into bed, he thought
about George Brock and his problems.
Earlier, when he and Brian had explained to Brock
Barry's reason for being behind his shop, Brock
hadn't bought it. And Sammy wasn't sure he had
either.

Had Brock brought all this trouble on
himself? Brock had fired Barry without proof
that he had stolen the missing iron. Sammy
also wondered what it would be like to have
your wife leave you. To be alone with nothing
but your work. To run a stop sign and kill
another person. Then to have accusations directed
against you by the community in which you live
and work. What guilt and shame this man must
harbor, thought Sammy. And then to have your
life threatened. A phone call, a written note...
cut-out letters. Ah, the letters. Was there a mean-

ingful message buried within the letters?

The young detective adjusted the sheet over his body. He squirmed until his back settled into the mattress's indentation. He relaxed, trying to think of nothing special. Just let it happen. Let what happen? he wondered. The letters are happening. You remember the letters, don't you? Yes, but what do they say? I need help, subconscious, thought Sammy to himself. The letters—what do they say?

You will die, came the answer. *You will die.* Yes, but when? Sammy wondered. No answer. How will I die? No answer. Why will I die? No answer. Where will I die? *In your shop*, came the answer. *You will die in your shop.*

Sammy's eyes popped open. He tried to cling onto the contents of the twilight level of sleep. His subconscious had delivered a message. He was sure of that. Yes. *You will die . . . in your shop. You will die in your shop!*

Sammy threw the sheet back. He rolled out of bed and hurried to his desk. The envelope was still on top. He spilled the letters onto a small pile and then deliberately turned them into their correct position. Then he formed the words. And the words formed the sentence—*you will die in your shop.* There were no letters left over. He had used them all.

He pictured somebody, in the dead of night, taking the Amish buggy. How would the thief haul it away? Hitch a horse to it? Load it into a

truck? Walk it away? He pictured someone leaning over to pick up the buggy shafts—the letters
falling from the shirt pocket onto the ground. That
could account for them being bunched together.
Were the letters meant for David Fisher? Was the
Amishman's life, too, being threatened? Or were
the buggy and the letters meant for George Brock?
Why? By whom?

Possibilities whirled around in Sammy's
head as he crawled back into bed. Because of what
had happened earlier that evening, Barry Bitner
was first on Sammy's suspect list. Next was Wally
Mills. But Sammy couldn't visualize Wally using
a phone call, a note, and cut-out letters to threaten
Brock. And two years after the accidental death
of Wally's wife? It didn't make sense. Like Wally's
son, Steve, said, "Life goes on."

Alex Austin was also on the suspect list.
She needed an Amish buggy, but she was no
threat to Brock. The conversation earlier in the
day indicated a friendship between the two.
Sammy turned on his left side and glanced toward the front window. Unless, he thought, there
was something else between Alex and George. He
tried to think of the possibilities. "Oh, well," he
yawned to the spirits of the night, "while Brian
visits Alex's restaurant in the morning, I'll pay
another visit to David Fisher."

The lack of large signs at Amish businesses was a statement of the Amish culture. Most Amish were involved in farming. However, the high prices and scarcity of farmland had forced some Amish into other occupations. Sammy had passed many lanes and converted barns along the road without realizing that Amish businesses lay within. Amish religion forbade competition. That meant no advertising. And except for small signs on mailboxes, word of mouth was the only boost Amish businesses received.

As the young detective pedaled off Lime Valley Road and drifted up the driveway, there was nothing to indicate that the converted barn was a carriage shop. Sammy leaned his bike against a tree. He half expected to see some of David's seven children playing about. He saw no one. He heard no one. Had David and his family gone away?

Sammy hurried to the shop and opened the door. He stepped inside...to an empty room. He couldn't believe it. The room was bare. Completely bare. All the buggy bodies, metal frames, and wheels were gone. The desk, the sewing machine, everything. Gone. Even the large rack with its rolls of cloth had disappeared. Sammy felt strange. Despite his skill and experience in problem solving, he couldn't come up with a rational explanation for what he saw. Why was the room stripped like this? Was David Fisher ripped off? He glanced down at the floor. At least there wasn't a dead body lying there.

Suddenly, a noise from the doorway made Sammy turn quickly. His blue eyes squinted at the bright light to bring the figure into focus. It was David Fisher, very much alive.

The Amishman was calm and appeared concerned at the strange expression on Sammy's face. "Sorry I didn't come so right away to the shop. Ach, you look befuddled. What's wrong?"

Sammy breathed a sigh of relief. "What happened here? Where is everything?"

"Climb the steps down onct and take a look."

"You mean you took everything down below?"

"Yah, we're having church service here on Sunday."

Sammy remembered the Amish did not have a church building. Instead, they had worship services in each other's homes every other Sunday. "Wow! Seems like a lot of work to clean out your shop like this."

"When the house is too small, we hold worship in the barn. It ain't any bother. Ach, it's only our turn about onct a year."

"Your congregation doesn't sit on the floor, do they?" asked Sammy, almost expecting a yes answer.

David smiled. "We may be plain, but we're not primitive. The wagon will fetch the benches, hymnals, and china tomorrow."

"It's a lot of work," said Sammy, visualizing the loading of the wagon, unloading, setting up the benches, taking the benches down, and reloading the wagon.

David nodded and took a deep breath. "We make ready for Sunday. We redd-up the house and sweep the floor down. My wife and the children already are getting the food list caught after."

"You have to feed the—? How many people are in your congregation?"

"Yah, we feed forty some. But everybody pitches in. It's pretty much social. Families being together, showing love for each other." David probed into Sammy's blue eyes and asked. "You English have something better?"

Sammy's eyes watered. "I can't think of anything that beats that," he offered truthfully. He wiped his eyes before the water became tears. "Hey, I just remembered why I'm here. I might have discovered the message in those letters you found outside."

The Amishman was still and waited.

"'I will kill you in your shop,' is what it said."

David paused, thinking it was a joke. When the serious concern on Sammy's face remained, David said, "Somebody wants to kill me here? Why?"

"Can you think of anyone who would want to harm you in any way?"

David shook his head. With a hint of a smile he said, "My wife gets after me some."

"I don't think the message was for you," said the young detective. "I believe whoever stole the buggy dropped the letters accidentally. I believe the message was for George Brock. He's received other warnings."

"So that's why he waited for you outside yesterday."

"Yeah."

"Some people aren't so much for him, yah?"

"Looks that way." Sammy didn't want to inquire whether David knew of the traffic accident involving the death of Wally Mills' wife. He might not have known about it, so why bring it all up again? "The police know about the threats. Brian and I are trying to help," he said as he headed out the door. "Well, I don't want to keep you from your work. See you later."

The Amishman waved as Sammy hopped on his bike and waved back.

David cupped his hands around his mouth and said loudly, "I must get my work caught up before my wife...Ach, here she comes."

The large, brick building had been a private home at one time. Since then, many attempts had been made to establish a business within its brick walls. Some were moderate successes. The last one, a restaurant, had been a failure. But now,

Alex Austin was going to make it a phenomenal success. She thought.

Her back was to the front door as she stepped away from the wall to admire the hanging quilt. Yes, it had just the right colors to accent the dining room. She had made the right choice in selecting this Amish quilt for her restaurant. It had cost more than she had intended to pay. But Alex accepted the fact that she had to spend money to make money.

With her mind on her bank balance and her back to the door, Alex didn't see or hear the man who quietly entered the restaurant. Nor was she aware of a young boy on a bike swinging around the side driveway to the back parking lot.

Brian tried to decide whether to brake his bike at the side of the building or to continue around to the back. Since the restaurant sat so close to the road, there was no room for parking in the front. But a wide driveway and a sign led the customers to a rear parking area. The teenage detective allowed his bike to coast down the driveway.

"All right," he said to himself as he rapidly approached a garage in front of him. He gave a lunge forward with his body, trying to stretch the coasting distance of his bike without having to pedal. It didn't work. He got off and walked the bike to the window.

Brian's enthusiasm and positive attitude told him the stolen buggy would be there in the garage. But he had to do this right. He glanced toward the restaurant's rear windows. His eyes darted from side to side, giving it his best secret agent mode of operation. He detected no one. He quietly leaned his "undercover vehicle" against the wooden building. But the stones under its wheels didn't respect the covert operation, and the bike slid to the asphalt. Loose stones prolonged the noise as they skidded along the surface of the parking lot.

Brian squeezed his eyes shut and hunched his shoulders as if trying to make himself invisible. He waited, then slowly opened his eyes and scanned the area. No one was watching. He was almost disappointed he had no audience. After all he was about to look in through the window and discover the stolen buggy.

Leaving his bike horizontally parked, the would-be detective stepped to the window. He cupped his hands around his face and peered inside. As he waited for his eyes to adjust to the near darkness, a familiar form took shape. Yes, he knew it! He knew it! It was there! The buggy was…not the missing buggy. The wheel rims were flat. No mistake. They were flat. Brian couldn't see the upholstery inside the carriage, but he didn't need to. He slowly backed away from the window.

Then from out of nowhere came a female voice tinged with anger. "Get out of here now, before I kill you."

CHAPTER EIGHT

B rian didn't need a second announcement. He grabbed his bike and was half way across the parking area when he heard another voice. "Put that knife down. You're not killing anybody." The voice, male this time, came through the open window of the restaurant.

When the young sleuth realized the threat was not directed at him, he spun his bike around and headed for the window. Someone's life was in danger all right. He wasn't going to ride away from that. He came in from the side so as not to be seen. With the bike propped against the building, he sneaked quietly to the window.

"Just go. Get out of here!" threatened the female voice.

"Look, I love you, Alex. Give me another chance," returned the male voice.

"How many chances have I already given you, Charlie? You spend more time with your airplane than you do with me. And look at those greasy hands. They're never clean."

"And I guess George Brock's hands are cleaner than mine. Is that it, Alex?"

"I'll date who I want, Charlie. Now go back to your airplane and leave me alone."

"Well, I have news for you. Your snowy white George won't be so clean when I get through with him."

Brian couldn't stand it any longer. He had heard that male voice before. It had to be Charlie Gordon from the Smoketown Airport. In the past year Charlie had taken Sammy and him for several aerial rides over the Bird-in-Hand area. Brian had to peek inside the window. His head tilted in from the corner.

A pair of surprised eyes returned his gaze.

"Brian, that you?" asked Charlie Gordon, coming closer to the window.

"Well, yeah," answered Brian, knowing there was no way out.

"What do you want?" asked Alex.

Brian had to think quickly. "Well, you...I was at the store yesterday when you bought a quilt. You said you were opening a restaurant."

"Yes...And?" said Alex.

"I just...just came by to see your restaurant."

"Well, I'm not open yet," snapped Alex, who was still feeling the sting of Charlie's remarks to her. "What are you doing at the window? Listening?"

Brian got all flustered. "N—no. I—I couldn't help myself. I took one look at this window and I said to myself, 'Brian, that would make a great take-out window.' "

"This isn't a fast-food restaurant," said Alex. "I'll be serving quality steaks here." And with that, she slammed the window shut. "Come back when I'm open," she yelled through the glass and then yanked down the blind.

"So the curtain came down on Alex's and Charlie's dramatic verbal attack," said Sammy after Brian had given him a vivid account of his morning visit to the restaurant. Sammy had returned from his visit with David Fisher, and as arranged, the boys had met at Brenda's Snack Counter. He had already explained to Brian about solving the message contained in the letters and about his visit to the carriage shop.

"Yep, shut the window right in my face," repeated Brian. "She was mad, but not at me. Sounds like Charlie's not on Alex's dating list anymore."

"But George Brock is," added Sammy. "From what you just told me, I'd say we might have another person who wants Mr. Brock out of the picture."

Brian grabbed Sammy's arm. "Hey, since Charlie loves Alex so much, he might even steal a buggy for her. Right, Sammy?"

"But you said the buggy you saw in the garage had flat wheel rims."

Brian released the hold on his friend's arm. "I've been thinking about that. Couldn't they have switched wheels?"

Sammy frowned and sat up straight on the stool. "Could be," he said as Brenda set the hot dogs and small paper plates of sauerkraut before the boys.

"You boys look real hungry," said Brenda as she picked up their money from the counter. "You must be working on a big case."

Brian nodded. His mouth was so full, he couldn't utter a word.

"Brenda," said Sammy, "do you know whether Alex Austin and George Brock have been dating long?"

Brenda's eyes glanced up and to the right as she pondered the question. "Just a week or so, I'd say. I heard they first dated after Brock did some metal work for her at the restaurant. Is that important to the case you're working on?"

"No, I don't think so," said Sammy, finally taking a bite of his hot dog and topping it off with sauerkraut. Even as he said the words, he had doubts. People had killed for love before, he thought to himself. Charlie could be trying to eliminate the competition.

"Hey, I have to go," said Brenda, interrupting Sammy's thoughts. "Stop in sometime when

I'm not so busy." With that, she was off to the cash register to deposit the boys' money. Then she hurried to join the others, serving the standing-room-only customers.

With his mouth now empty, Brian leaned toward Sammy, without tilting the stool this time. "If it's Charlie who's after Brock, do you think he'll kill him?"

Sammy wiped his mouth with a napkin and stepped down from the stool. "No, but he might try to rough him up a bit to keep him away from Alex." Sammy's blue eyes paused. Deep thoughts churned through his head. Then he pulled on his friend's arm. "Come on, Brian. Let's pay a visit to the welding shop. We need to make an important decision."

The temperature was in the eighties as Sammy and Brian pedaled through the rolling hills of Lime Valley. Fluffy white clouds backed up farms with fields of wall-to-wall corn and alfalfa. Since dairy farming was the primary business of most Amish, cows could be seen dotting the meadows near the barns.

Every twist and turn of the road offered a new view. To the right, Sammy relished the sight of the recently restored covered bridge that still lingered in the modern world. He thought some bygone values probably needed restoring, too.

On the side of the road up ahead, two bare-foot Amish boys had homemade brooms which were stacked in their wooden wagon. A small sign posted on the nearby tree informed the passing public that the brooms were for sale. Both boys wore wide-brimmed, yellow straw hats. Suspenders, strapped over pastel blue shirts, held up their black cotton trousers.

It was hard for tourists to resist stopping and purchasing an "Amish" broom. The excited tourists could get a close-up look at real Amish children. And for the price of a broom, they might dare ask questions about their culture.

As they passed the Amish boys, Sammy and Brian smiled and waved. Up ahead across the bridge, Sammy could see his uncle's farm on his left and David Fisher's carriage shop on his right. They were headed for the welding shop, so the teenage detectives turned left at the bridge. They rode along the brim of the road, following the creek until they saw Brock's truck.

"Hey, he's here," said Brian.

"Yeah, but the garage door is open," said Sammy.

Sammy had advised Brock to keep all doors closed and locked when he was working inside. Had somebody gotten to Brock already? Were the boy detectives too late? Sammy quickly propped his bike against the truck and ran to the opening. Brian laid his bike on the ground, figuring that's where it would end up anyway. He followed his friend in through the open doorway.

The boys flinched back. Flashes of light and a spray of hot sparks flew up from behind two tall and heavy metal plates and lit up the area. And then it was over. Semi-darkness returned. Sammy held his ground, but Brian retreated, tripping over the ends of iron rods. To keep himself from falling, he grabbed at a rope dangling at the door frame. The rope and its anchor broke loose, sending Brian to the floor—directly beneath the falling garage door. The heavy wooden door creaked as it started to descend. Brian held on to the rope, and when the slack was gone, the door stopped—inches above him.

"Don't let go of the rope!" shouted Sammy as he grabbed it and pulled.

Brian rolled away and got to his feet. Together they raised the door and secured the rope to a metal pipe.

"Everybody all right? What happened?" asked George Brock, hurrying from the back of the shop. The metal face shield worn by welders was perched atop his head.

Brian glanced at Sammy, expecting his friend to explain away his misadventure. Instead, Sammy brushed his hair back and raised his eyebrows, giving Brian the you're-on-your-own look.

Luckily for Brian, Brock noticed the brass anchor hook on the floor. "Oh, the hook came off again," said Brock as he picked it up and threw it on the nearby desk. "I need bigger screws to hold it." He watched as Brian rubbed his hands over his clothing, dislodging some particles of loose dirt. "Sorry, did you hurt yourself?"

Before Brian could answer, Sammy said, "You're the one that could be hurt. You have this door open. You're here alone. The person threatening you can come in here and..."

"I know. I'm sorry. But it gets hot in here when I'm welding." He pointed to the metal face protector. "And wearing this makes it worse." He motioned toward his desk. "You boys wait over there. I'll be with you in a couple of minutes. I'm making a feed bin hopper for a farmer. I have to weld four heavy plates together." With that, he plodded back, picked up the welding torch, and disappeared behind the metal.

Sparks flew as the welding torch started a seam, joining two very large and heavy steel plates together. The bright bursts of light that spit dancing sparks reminded the boys of fireworks.

Sammy was amazed at how easily anyone could enter the shop, sneak up behind Brock, and hit him over the head. Even with a welding torch in his hand, George would not be prepared for a sneak attack from the rear.

Brian saw the golf bag leaning against the wall behind Brock's desk. He nudged his partner. "Hey, anyone could come in here, grab a club, and hit Brock over the head."

"There are a lot of potential weapons all over this shop," replied Sammy as he eyed several cylinders of compressed gases, pieces of iron rods, and long heavy wrenches.

Brian went around the desk and pulled a club from the leather bag. "Probably use the nine iron," he said. "That's the one I'd use if I was going to clobber someone." He raised the club and brought it down near Sammy's head.

Sammy quickly stepped aside, not quite trusting Brian's attempt at a live demonstration. "Brian, those are real clubs. You're not at The Village Greens miniature golf course."

"Hey, this isn't a bad set of clubs." Brian held the nine iron and swung at an imaginary golf ball. "This club was made for me. It's a perfect fit." He started to swing again but saw George Brock walking toward them. He quickly slipped the club back into the bag with the others.

"Golf is the only joy I get out of life these days," said George sadly. "Those clubs and the people I work with at the hospital are the only friends I have."

"I understand you do volunteer work at the hospital," said Sammy.

"Yeah, it's part of my probation." Brock looked sheepishly at the boys. "I guess by this time you know about the traffic accident. A woman died as a result of it, and I was put on three years probation with public service."

Sammy nodded. "That enlarges our list of suspects. Wally Mills and *Charlie Gordon*." Sammy watched for a reaction from Brock at the mention of Charlie's name.

Brock shrugged it off. "If the truth be known, most people around here would like to see me dead." He sat behind his desk and cleaned his hands with a new rag from the desk drawer. Keeping his eyes on the rag, he said, "After all, I killed Wally Mills' wife. Maybe I do deserve to die."

So that's it, thought Sammy. That's why the doors are open. His guilt is so strong, he's inviting someone to kill him. Sammy glanced at the dirt and grease that was coming off on the rag. If only guilt could be wiped away as easily, he thought.

Still staring at the rag, George announced, "I got another phone call this morning. The message was that I will die tomorrow." He threw the dirty rag at the desk and glanced at Sammy. "But I will not be forced out of my shop."

That was all Sammy had to hear. Now he realized what had to be done. Sammy told George about the cut-out letters that were found at the time the buggy was taken from the carriage shop. "I believe those cut-out letters were meant for you. Last night I discovered the threat those letters carried. It was the same as all of your warnings. You will be killed here. Why don't you let the police help you?"

"The police didn't find any prints but mine on the note. And they can't help me unless someone actually harms me." George stood and walked to Sammy, placing his hand on Sammy's shoulder. "I'm sure you boys can scare him off."

"Knowing where you will be killed," said Brian, "gives us an advantage. Right, Sammy?"

"Mr. Brock, you have two new friends, Brian and me. What we need to do is set up surveillance here at your shop, starting tomorrow morning."

A nervous smile appeared on George's face. "I've been thinking about that." He walked from the desk to the open doorway and pointed across the road toward the creek. "You could be on the other side of the stream out there. You know, pretending you're fishing."

"Yeah, right under the willow tree," said Brian. "We could watch the whole place from there," said Brian.

Sammy frowned, walked outside, and looked around. The others followed.

"I was thinking of being closer to the shop," said Sammy, making a final survey of the area. "But the idea of fishing could be our cover." He grinned. "Yes, I like it. And besides, there is a way we can be under that willow tree *and* be over here at the same time."

CHAPTER NINE

"Wow, this zoom lens is great!" said Sammy as he leaned out of his bedroom window. The camera was pointed left toward the Junction. Words came into focus as he adjusted the camera. "I can even read the small sign on the door." He carefully moved away from the window, lowered the camera, and said, "Joyce, welcome back to the Sammy and Brian detective team."

Joyce Myers was fifteen years old. She, too, was a member of the Brain Teasers Club at school and had helped the boys solve the case of *Amish Justice*. That case involved murder on a nearby farm. Joyce was wearing a T-shirt and jeans. Her large hazel eyes and oval face were enhanced by her short brown hair.

She reached for her camera and smiled. "What do I have to do to become a permanent member of the team?"

"Ah, so you want to be a detective," said Brian, standing by the empty rocking chair. "Normally it takes years of intense training and experience," he said with a dramatic flair. "You must be able to detect the smallest clue. You must have the ability to face the villains and show no fear. You must—"

"Brian," interrupted Sammy.

"Okay, okay," said Brian, taking his dramatics in another direction. "Joyce, to be one of us you must reclaim your throne." He pointed to the padded rocking chair that Sammy's mother had given them for Joyce to use when she had helped on a previous case. It was in this rocker that, with a couple of old photographs, she had detected a clue that was a key to solving the case.

Joyce smiled as she backed into the rocker and rested her camera on her lap. She wiggled, allowing her body to reshape the cushions and announce she was back. She pushed her toes against the floor. The rocking chair creaked along with the floor boards. "It's old enough to be a throne," she said, looking at Brian, "but it can't be a throne. Thrones don't rock."

"Yeah, well, they should have rocked," said Brian. "You ever see those old painting of kings and queens? Those sour faces? Well, if the thrones had been rockers, they would have big smiles on their faces."

"In that case," said Joyce with a melodramatic tone of authority, "I reclaim my throne. And

I promise that I shall use my problem solving abilities—" She raised her camera over her head. "—and my camera to help bring the bad guys and girls to justice."

"That sounds pretty official to me," said Brian, glancing at his partner. "Right, Sammy?"

Even with serious business at hand, Sammy was in a mellow mood. He liked Joyce. He enjoyed being with her at school in the Brain Teasers Club. She was smart, challenging, and always friendly. Her observation skills, input at brainstorming sessions, and knowledge of photography would be an extra bonus for them all.

To everybody's surprise, including himself, Sammy said, "Brian, I think it's time you gave Joyce the oath of admittance into our club." It wasn't often that Sammy gave Brian the reigns to flaunt his humor.

Both Brian and Joyce glanced at Sammy.

"What?" asked Brian, surprised at his friend's remark.

Sammy's blue eyes sparkled, and one even winked as he sat behind his oak desk. He folded his hands on the desk and leaned forward. He was now ready to enjoy seeing how Brian would get through this one.

"Well, yeah,...sure...absolutely. We can't forget the oath that makes Joyce's membership official...can we?"

"Go ahead, Brian," said Joyce, adding pressure to the challenge Sammy had presented to Brian.

"Well, okay." Brian's mind was racing. "Raise your right hand and repeat after me. I promise never to chew gum when I'm interviewing a suspect. I will...never point my camera at anyone unless it's loaded. I will...strive to become at least half as smart as Sammy and Brian, Bird-in-Hand's great detectives, known the world over for their...I promise when at Brenda's Snack Counter I will always order hot dogs with sauerkraut...on the side. I will remember never to tilt the stool—"

"How do you expect me to repeat all of that?" asked Joyce, grinning and playing along. "I can't remember it all."

"Just...just...When I'm finished just say, 'I promise.' "

Joyce closed her eyes and faked a yawn. "I will, I promise...if I'm still awake."

Brian frowned then continued. He was trying to give Sammy his money's worth. "I promise never to accuse anyone of a crime unless I have proof." Brian twisted his head toward Sammy and grinned. He continued. "When I am brainstorming with Brian and Sammy, I will always listen to and accept Brian's ideas. I will—"

"Okay, I promise," said Joyce.

"But I'm not finished yet."

Joyce's arm flopped down into her lap. "My arm's getting tired."

"Lack of energy, huh," said Brian. "I'm sorry, but that disqualifies you."

"That's not lack of energy, Brian," said Sammy joining in. "That's using common sense. She's smart enough to know that nobody has the energy needed to stand up to your verbal professionalism."

Brian stared at Sammy. "Hey, that's true all right." He looked back at Joyce who by this time was giggling. "I apologize for being slow at recognizing your smartness, your majesty." He bowed, reached for her hand, and raised it to his face.

"Brian," said Sammy, "if you're getting ready to kiss her hand, forget it."

"But it's clean," said a wide-eyed Brian.

Sammy couldn't hold back the snicker any longer. Soon all three teenagers filled the room with laughter.

But it didn't last long. Not with Sammy controlling the business at hand. The mood changed quickly. Sammy brought Joyce up to date with the facts on David Fisher's missing buggy, the cut-out letters and their message, and the other threats on George Brock's life. He recounted how they found Barry Bitner among the trees at the welding shop. Brian told of his visit to the restaurant and the conversation at the opened window. They even went over the list of suspects

As Joyce listened, the rocking chair picked up speed. She tried not to jump to conclusions, especially where lack of evidence was concerned. Her first impulse was to believe that these were two separate mysteries. After all, how could a missing buggy be connected to death threats against a welder? She did find it odd though that the same people were connected to both crimes.

Brian had flopped back on the bed. He had nodded his head at the ceiling to confirm each statement made by Sammy.

When Sammy's discussion was over, Joyce stopped rocking and took a deep breath. "Okay, how can I help? You told me to bring my camera with me when you called. From what you just said, I'm guessing we're going to do a stakeout. Am I close?"

"Right on," said Sammy. "Starting tomorrow we're going to keep our eyes and your camera on Brock's welding shop. If anybody is out to get Mr. Brock, we'll be there. We'll continue the search for the buggy later. Right now, George Brock's life is more important."

"With luck you might catch the guilty person on film," added Brian, flipping himself up from the bed.

"Before or after he kills Mr. Brock?" asked Joyce.

Brian crossed over to the desk. "Show her the diagram you made."

Sammy unfolded the paper as Joyce left the rocker and joined Brian by the desk. "This drawing is a bird's eye view of the welding shop and the surrounding area.

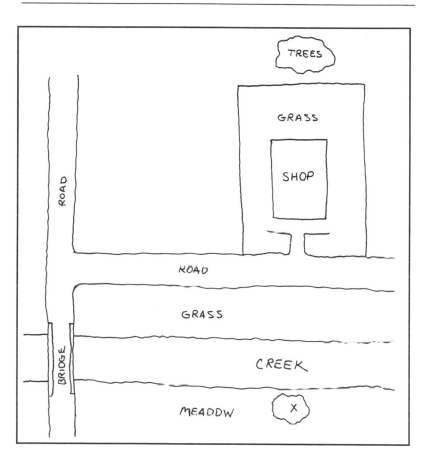

"This rippled oval near the top," continued Sammy, "represents a bunch of trees that are at the edge of the field behind the welding shop."

"That's where you found Barry Bitner hiding," said Joyce.

"Right." Sammy continued to slide his finger down the paper. "This rectangle is the welding shop. You can see there's open space around it. There's a parking area in front with a grass area that extends to the road. These two parallel lines going across the paper represent the road in front."

Brian was getting impatient. He poked his finger at the sketch and declared, "This is about fifteen feet of grass on the other side of the road. And this is the creek. And this little circle on the other side of the creek is a willow tree. And the X under the tree is us—fishing."

Sammy nodded to confirm that his partner had gotten it right. "Joyce, we want you to photo-graph, with your zoom lens, any car or person that goes near the shop. The shop doors will be locked. We have signals arranged with Mr. Brock. If anyone comes to the door and everything is okay, he will leave the door open. If he senses any danger, he will pull the blind down in the window next to the door."

Brian went to the bedroom window and peered out as though looking for spies. His eyes scanned up and down Main Street. After all, he thought, this is an undercover operation. Great harm would be done to our plan if the guilty party got wind of our surveillance strategy.

He stepped back from the window. He didn't want to be in the direct line of fire should the criminals out there in the cruel world decide to eliminate him. And just in case they had seen him at the window, he stuck his hand behind his back. He wanted them to know he was ready to draw his weapon should the need arise. And the need was now. Somebody...was...lurking...in the shadows...across the street. Brian quickly swung his hand around from his back and pointed his "loaded" finger directly at...the...woman.

Sammy interrupted Brian's James Bond impersonation. "So wear old clothes and old sneakers," said Sammy. "If George Brock is in any danger, we may need to swim or wade across the creek quickly. We won't have time to ride to the bridge, cross over, and come back up the road."

"I have old clothes," said Joyce, "but I don't have a fishing pole."

"You don't need one. We're each going to use a long stick with a stone tied to a string. That way we'll look like we're fishing, but we won't catch any. We can't afford to be bothered with fish. We need to keep our full attention focused on the welding shop."

"How about lunch?" asked Joyce. "We need to eat."

"That's all taken care of," said Sammy. "My mother's going to pack us a picnic basket."

"Hey, no egg salad sandwiches. I hate them," said Brian, over his shoulder. However, his eyes were still fixed on the attractive female, who now was writing something in a small notebook.

"How about lobster tail?" said Joyce, smiling at Sammy.

"How about bologna sandwiches?" replied Sammy.

Joyce was expecting a humorous reply from Brian. When none came, she lifted herself and her camera from the rocker and sneaked to the window. She followed Brian's gaze to the figure across the street. The woman appeared to be looking around, trying to decide in which direction to go.

Sammy's curiosity led him also to the sparse crowd of two at the window. "What's the attraction?" he asked.

"You know that lady?" asked Joyce, squeezing Brian's arm.

Brian looked up at Sammy. "Yeah, we know her," he said. "It's Alex Austin."

CHAPTER TEN

George Brock opened the door and stepped out into the fresh, early morning air. He nodded at the three teenagers fishing on the opposite side of the creek across the road. It was a natural thing for a businessman to do under normal circumstances. Of course these were *not* normal circumstances. George was tense. He knew this was the day.

Joyce was sitting on a blanket with her knees bent up together, acting as a sturdy support for her camera. She knew it was not wise to hand-hold a camera fitted with a heavy zoom lens. Any slight movement of the camera caused the magnified image to streak across the film, blurring the picture.

"Is it working? Can you see George?" asked Brian.

"Sure can," said Joyce. "And I took his picture to check the camera. It's working."

What wasn't working was the blind spot that the camera couldn't see. Joyce could see all along the back fields on either side of the welding shop. But she couldn't see the small gathering of trees directly behind the building. If anybody sneaked down from the trees, they wouldn't be seen. However, to get to the trees, the person would need to cross from either side, along the fields. That, Joyce's camera would see and record.

Sammy watched as George Brock disappeared back into the shop and closed the door. He made a last minute check of his two fishing buddies. Yes, they were wearing old clothes. Yes, three long sticks were propped on the bank in front of each of them with the slack in the string being teased by the water's current. And yes, to anyone passing, they were just three teenagers enjoying the morning and trying to catch fish.

Brian looked out from under his father's old fishing hat and frowned. "It's a great day for fishing. Too bad we're not."

"Yes, we are," said Joyce. "We're fishing for the person who might harm Mr. Brock. And to me that's more exciting then pushing a little worm on a hook and then hoping it looks appetizing to a cute little fish who swam away from its mother and—"

"Ah, Joyce," said Brian, whining, "you just took the joy out of fishing."

"Speaking of fishing," said Sammy, "What do you think Alex Austin was trying to catch last night out on Main Street?"

Joyce glanced at Sammy. "I'd like to know what she was writing in her notebook. What did she see that was worth jotting down?"

"She's odd," said Brian. "I knew it as soon as she shut the window on me."

"Hey, here comes a car," said Sammy. "Get ready."

"I'm always ready," growled Brian.

Joyce focused the camera on the car as it slowed, pulled over to their side of the road, and stopped. The driver lowered his window and yelled something at the trio.

Brian stood and waved his arms as though he was flagging down a train. "It's Fred, my next door neighbor. Hi, Fred!" shouted Brian.

"I thought it was you, Brian," yelled Fred. "I recognized your father's fishing hat. What are you doing, fishing?"

"No, we're only pre—" Brian stopped suddenly as he realized what he was doing. "Yeah, Fred, we're fishing," he yelled. "See you later."

The car window closed and the car pulled out and continued down the road.

"You see, it was a natural thing," said Brian. "A friend sees us and says hello. We say hello back, and he goes away. What's more natural than that?"

The other two had their heads down with their hands covering their faces.

Brian plowed on. "What can I say? I have a face that's known all over. People see me from two blocks away and they say, 'Hey, there's Brian.' People are drawn to me. I have a lot of friends. I can't help it. People love me. That's just the kind of guy I am."

The laughter burst through Joyce's hands first, followed closely by Sammy's reserved chuckle.

"Just remember, Brian, we're supposed to be undercover," said Sammy. "Try not to draw attention to yourself."

"Boys, be alert. We might have something," said Joyce. She pointed her camera in the general direction of a dark figure standing in the back field.

Sammy squinted his blue eyes. "It's an Amishman." His eyes returned to Joyce. "You don't have to take his picture unless you want a photo of an Amishman standing at the edge of his corn field."

"I think I will," she said.

The camera centered on the man.

"Get it quick. He's walking away," said Brian.

"*Quickly,*" said Joyce as her camera panned left, following the Amishman. "Brian, you need the adverb form. Get it *quickly.*"

Brian just gazed at Joyce. Finally he said, "Okay, teacher, but now you missed the shot because you weren't *quickly* enough." Brian grinned.

"I got three shots of the Amishman," said Joyce. "One standing, two moving."

"You are fast," said Sammy.

"Yeah, she can be quick quickly," said Brian to prove he knew the difference between an adjective and an adverb.

Sammy and Joyce moaned.

"You know what I always say," continued Brian. "When in doubt use both of them."

"This could be a long day," said Sammy as he scanned the quiet countryside. Behind him were several cows staking their claims to the meadow. Back to his left was his uncle's farm. He could see Aunt Barbara near the house, moving around in the vegetable garden.

A car passed slowly over the concrete bridge and hesitated before making a right turn. It was coming their way. The car's occupants were evidently searching for something. The car continued up the road, paying no attention to the three teenagers fishing.

The camera clicked.

"Out-of-state license," said Brian. "Probably looking for the Amish."

Joyce pulled her eye away from the camera. "Brian, you're too modest. I bet they heard that 'Brian, the Great Boy Detective,' was in the area. If your father's hat hadn't fallen down over your ears and eyes, they would have been over here, hounding you for your autograph."

Brian raised the hat so it rested on his ears and, without missing a beat, said, "Yeah, well, there are times when my job comes first, and my personal life must take a back seat. It is times like these that my fans and I must suffer. But humility and dedication to the job compels me to clinch my teeth and put my feelings aside." He ended his theatrics by removing his hat, placing it over his heart, and bowing his head.

"Wow, what an actor," teased Joyce. "I'm surprised the fish didn't pop up out of the water and applaud."

Sammy interrupted the duo's patter by pointing toward the shop. "Looks like we have competition. Someone else is scrutinizing the area."

"Oh, isn't he a darling," said Joyce as a medium-sized, light brown dog sniffed its way around the bushes in front of the welding shop.

Before anyone could comment further, a car came up from the right and pulled in at the shop. With the sudden intrusion, the dog lost interest in the bushes and scampered around the side of the building.

The camera clicked, recording the car and its license number. The film advanced to the next frame—ready to freeze the next piece of history. Especially if it pertained to the shortening of Mr. Brock's life.

The passenger-side door opened and a woman slid out. She carried a cake-size white box in her hands. She rounded the front of the car and headed for the office door. The driver remained in the car.

"Hey, that must be Alex Austin bringing a cake to her boyfriend," whispered Brian.

The camera clicked.

Sammy's thoughts went immediately to Alex Austin as a suspect. If she was the person responsible for the death threats, now would be the time for her to act. And the box she carried would be the method. Poisoned food. Alex could be long gone before George ate the food and died. Or did she intend to stay and watch him die? But what about the driver of the car? He could be an accomplice. Or maybe he doesn't know what she is about to do. Before he could explore more possibilities, a voice broke through his concentration.

"I can see her face. It's Dottie Price," said Joyce, still glued to the camera and clicking a shot. "She's delivering barbecued chicken that the Bird-in-Hand Fire Company sells every year. Someone always drives her around every year so she can make the deliveries."

The three sleuths watched as Dottie tried the locked door. She moved over to the window and peeked in. She returned to the door and knocked this time. She waited, still balancing the box in her one hand.

"Mr. Brock is probably welding and can't hear her," said Brian. "Think we should do something?"

"No, we don't do anything," replied Sammy. "We're not even here, remember?"

Dottie and the box returned to the waiting car. It backed up and continued down the road.

Joyce checked the number of shots that were left on the roll of film. "If I know Dottie," said Joyce, "she'll make other deliveries then stop by again on the way back."

The sound of the departing car was replaced by the metallic crunching of buggy wheels on the asphalt road. Amish buggies were not a rare sight on these back country roads. What was rare was *this* Amish buggy. Instead of being pulled by a horse, it was being pulled by an Amishman—walking backwards.

When the Amishman had walked the buggy directly in front of the welding shop, he stopped. He turned around, grabbed the shafts, and pulled the buggy up to the building.

The zoom lens probed for composition and detail. When it was there, the camera clicked. "This is great," came the voice from behind the camera. "I can add these to my other Amish pictures."

"You ought to write a book about the Amish," said Brian. "With your ability to write and the great photos you take, it'd be a great book."

Joyce Myers had more than a reputation as a problem solver. Her creative writing ability and her skill in photography were well known. Not only had she learned how to get the most from her camera, but she also operated a well-equipped darkroom.

Joyce had not come into this world with a little camera in her one hand and a pencil and paper in the other. She developed these skills over the years. They were presents from Joyce to herself. For Joyce, the gift of learning was the best present of all. And it was a gift that only she could give to herself.

She smiled at Brian's comment and peered through the camera. She spoke without missing a click. "Anybody can write. Writing is just talk written down." Joyce's smile widened. "Brian, you could write volumes."

Brian opened his mouth to say something funny, but instead, he glanced up at the clouds. Maybe someday, he thought, I'll write a book about the adventures of Sammy and Brian. "Nah," he said to himself.

After parking the buggy, the Amishman moved to the window, glanced in, and waved. But instead of going inside, he shuffled off to the side of the building. Apparently finding a friend, the dog reappeared and sniffed at the Amishman. The Amishman stopped, reached over, and petted the friendly animal.

The camera clicked.

"I wonder if the dog is the *Amishman's* best friend?" asked Brian.

"No," answered Sammy, "the Amishman's best friend is his horse...next to his family and religion."

The three young detectives watched in silence as the man headed for the rear of the property and the trees and the corn field beyond.

The camera clicked once more.

Fifteen minutes later, as boredom was starting to set in, a faint hum was heard over the rippling of the stream. The droning got louder and louder until a low-flying plane was seen skimming over the area.

"Must be crop dusting," said Brian.

Before Joyce could raise her camera to get a shot, the plane disappeared. And just as fast, a car appeared, slowed in front of them, then speeded down the road and turned left over the bridge. The teenage detective swung her camera in the direction of the car and snapped a shot.

"Wow, he was traveling," said Sammy.

"All I saw was a streak of yellow," added Brian.

"It was his shirt," said Joyce. "I did see that much through the camera.

"Hum," muttered Sammy as Jack Mills came to mind. Jack, his friend of "a thousand and one" yellow shirts.

Then without warning, Sammy's "hum" was replaced by a deafening boom.

The explosion produced a rumble and a roar. It tore at the air and made the ground tremble. A thunderous crash was heard as the welding shop was ripped apart. Its walls collapsed, sending parts of the roof crashing to the ground.

The force of the blast pushed the three teen-agers backwards, propelling them into creative gymnastic routines they hadn't rehearsed. The camera separated from Joyce's hand. Brian's father's hat went into orbit, while Brian skimmed over the ground. The tumbling picnic basket opened and laid out its menu of food, forgetting to spread the cloth cover first. The three bicycles survived untouched because they were lying on the grass. Sammy's uncoordinated body somehow managed to land in one piece, among the chunks of cinder block that rained down from above.

Even the creek was not immune to the horrible intrusion to the peaceful countryside. The blast stirred the stream and sprayed a mixture of water and dust over the gasping teenagers. A fragment of metal embedded itself into the willow tree. Its leaves and birds were catapulted into the air on a premature flight.

And then silence...except for the occasional sparks heard as they flew from twisted electric wires.

The stunned detectives were trying to make the trip back to reality. They lay there in dis-belief, their ears ringing. Then when they assured themselves and each other that no bones were broken, they stood and looked at what had been George Brock's welding shop. Only the rear of the shop remained standing.

"Come on! Let's get over there!" shouted Sammy as he and the others raced back to the bank. They waded through the water, crawled up the muddy bank, and crossed the road.

Up close, the scene was even more frightening. The large space that used to be a welding shop was mostly in shambles. Only parts of the back walls stood. The storeroom that once stocked George's wrought iron crafts was gone. The machinery and raw stock that remained were heavily damaged. The force of the explosion twisted metal, broke glass, and started fires. Several damaged cylinders had leaked gasses and caused secondary explosions. These in turn started small fires among the piles of debris. The only structure that remain intact after the explosion was the large feed bin hopper, sitting six feet from the back wall. Pieces of the roof had come to rest atop the metal hopper.

Sammy was looking for the remains of George Brock. Smoke, dust, and heat encased the young sleuth as he wandered among the rubble. His clothes, still dripping wet from wading the stream, insulated him from the intense heat. He moved some rubble to check for a body beneath. He zigzagged his way through the debris listening for any sounds that would indicate that George Brock might still be alive.

As he neared the hopper, he heard a metallic sound.

Someone was inside the feed bin, knocking, trying to be heard.

Sammy waved his arms. "Back here! Back here!"

When Joyce and Brian reached the hopper, Sammy had already removed several pieces of splintered lumber. It took all three to slide the torn and bent metal roofing aside. Finally one side of the six-foot-high hopper was cleared.

Brian jumped, grabbed the top edge of the bin, and pulled himself up. "It's partly open on top." He glanced down and saw Brock, dazed, his hand weakly striking at the metal wall.

"It's Mr. Brock. He's alive," said Brian. Sliding over the top edge, he lowered himself, being careful not to land on George or the welding torch and cylinder by his side. "He's wearing the face shield," said Brian. "Should I lift it up so he can get some air?"

"Yeah," said Sammy, "but don't move him. Somebody must have called 911. I hear sirens. Help's on the way"

Joyce worked her way around piles of burning debris, through the smoke, and staggered back to the road. She was now in a position to direct help to George Brock.

Seconds later, cars and fire trucks filled the narrow country road. A small group of onlookers gathered and watched as the fire chief established command.

Because of Joyce Myers' suggestion and his own assessment of the situation, the fire chief called for the rescue unit out of Ronks. He sent three firemen back to the hopper to transport the victim out of harm's way. Other firemen prepared to bring the small fires under control.

Stumbling out through the smoke, Sammy and Brian welcomed the fresh air. They were quickly directed by the fire chief to join Joyce and the curious spectators behind the yellow caution tape.

"Hey, Sammy, you kids all right?" yelled a voice from behind. Detective Ben Phillips came running from across the road and anxiously pulled the three teens aside.

"Yeah, we're okay," said Sammy. He pointed to one of the fire trucks. "The firemen have Mr. Brock over there. I think he's okay."

Phillips was pleased to see George Brock alive. "I was contacted when they realized it was Brock's Welding Shop that was the object of the 911 call."

Several firemen acknowledged the four as they approached the truck. And at the same time, the ambulance, sirens whining, came to a careful stop near the crowd.

Brock was seated, holding a blanket tightly around his wet body. He glanced up at Sammy, gave a grim smile, and said, "You will die in your shop. Those letters lied. Didn't they?" His face lost the smile. "I'm too dead to die."

"You'll be all right, George," said Phillips as the paramedics placed an oxygen mask over his face and prepared him for the trip to the hospital.

As the stretcher was lifted, something fell to the ground, making a metallic sound. George lifted the mask. "My keys. Give me my keys," he said. He had lost his business. He didn't want to lose his keys.

One of the paramedics pressed the set of keys into George's hand and replaced the oxygen mask. "Here they are. I know how important it is for a man to have his keys and his wallet."

At the mention of the wallet, George shifted his body and slid his empty hand over the slight bulge in his back pants pocket. Then he relaxed back on the stretcher. He was now ready for the ride to the hospital.

"He looks okay to me," said Brian. "Why the hospital?"

"You can't always tell by looking," replied the detective. "He might have internal bleeding. The hospital is equipped to run tests and take x-rays if necessary." He pulled a notebook from his pocket. "You ready to tell me what happened here?"

The trio described their experiences since they had arrived earlier that morning. When they finished, Phillips closed the notebook and returned it to his pocket.

Another car joined the already jammed area. Three police officers got out and advanced to the smoldering rubble. Two male, one female. The female was holding a camera and a leather bag.

"Hi, Marlene," said Joyce. She had met the corporal while helping Sammy and Brian on a previous case. Marlene had even invited Joyce to take a tour of the police station darkroom. Joyce had learned a lot from that visit.

"Hello, Joyce," replied Marlene. "How's the photography going?"

"Oh, my camera!" yelled Joyce. She took off, heading for the creek. "I'll be back!" she hollered over her shoulder.

Marlene was puzzled.

"She left her camera across the way," added Sammy.

Marlene glanced at Detective Phillips. "Okay if we start now?"

Phillips looked at the fire chief who nodded his head. "It's all yours," said Phillips. He watched as the Record and Identification Unit went about the task of collecting, identifying, and recording evidence.

Ben Phillips walked over to what had been healthy bushes growing in front of the shop. Those that remained were in shreds. He stood silently, looking at the crime scene. His attention went immediately to a small crater in the ground.

"That's where the buggy was," said Sammy.

CHAPTER ELEVEN

The eight-by-ten, black and white photographs were spread across Sammy's bed. Brian's "space" was occupied by George Brock standing by an opened door, Dottie Price carrying a box, and an Amishman pulling a buggy. The additional photos filled in the rows that ended at the pillow. The last picture showed the rubble of what had been a welding shop.

A bomb. Who would have suspected a bomb?

Whoever was behind this terrible scheme had planned carefully.

The seven-o'clock brainstorming meeting started with little enthusiasm. A crime had been committed, and the trio could not prevent it. Now they had little to work with. They had their list of suspects. They had their memory of the morning. And they had some still pictures taken during the stakeout. Thankfully, Joyce's camera had not been damaged during the explosion or they wouldn't even have those. The teenage detectives had nothing that even hinted at the guilty party.

The three lackluster detectives stood along the bed, hovering over the picture enlargements. Their only hope was that somewhere in these photos was a piece of evidence.

"What surprises me the most was that, one, the threat was carried out, and two, that the weapon was a bomb," said Sammy as he continued to scan the photos.

"And it happened right before our eyes," added Brian. "The bomb was put there, and we missed it."

Joyce picked up the picture of the Amishman pulling the buggy. "We didn't miss it if the bomb was in the buggy."

Sammy took the photo from Joyce's hand and shook his head. "I can't believe the bomb was in the buggy."

"Yeah, an Amishman isn't even on our list of suspects," said Brian.

Joyce leaned closer to the other enlargements on the bed. "His face doesn't show up much in any of these pictures."

"If the bomb wasn't in the buggy, why was the hole in the ground there?" asked Brian. "You think it was planted in the ground before this morning?"

"I don't know much about explosives, but

from the shape of the crater, I'd say the explosive device was either on the ground or above it."

Brian pointed his finger at the photo of the car crossing the bridge. "So the bomb could have been thrown from that car and rolled under the buggy."

Joyce shook her head. "No way. The yellow shirt guy was the only one in the car, and he was driving. He was sitting in the car on our side of the road. And we didn't see him deliver a hook shot over the car."

"Oh, I know," said Brian. "It was dropped from the plane."

"That's a possibility," said Sammy. "By the time we looked up at the plane, the device could had been released. And when the bomb landed near the buggy, our eyes were on the plane."

With some excitement in her voice, Joyce added, "Yeah, he was aiming for the roof but missed."

Sammy continued the thought. "But the bomb didn't explode as soon as it hit the ground. There had to be a long fuse."

"Will the test results from the police lab in Harrisburg tell us how it exploded?" asked Brian.

"Yeah, I think so," said Sammy. "But if the bomb *was* detonated using a fuse, we can't prove it was thrown from the plane."

Brian slipped his hands into his pockets and moped over to the desk. "So all we have so far is a big bunch of nothing. Right, Sammy?"

Sammy flung the picture he was holding back onto the bed. "I did solve one mystery though," he said and walked to the window.

"What mystery?" asked Joyce as she, too, abandoned the bed, the photos, and the apparent dead end they represented. She slipped into the rocker.

Sammy nodded to Main Street below. "I know what Alex Austin was doing down there last night." He displayed a piece of paper from his pocket. "She was delivering invitations to a free buffet at her restaurant."

"Hey, that's where they have different kinds of food on a long table and you serve yourself," said Brian.

"And you can eat all you want," added Joyce.

"It's free? Why would she do that?" asked Brian and sat in Sammy's chair.

"Advertisement," said Sammy.

"Hey, that's smart," said Joyce. "Alex knows that tourists are always asking where there's a good place to eat. So she invites business people from the area to a delicious meal. They get to know her and her restaurant. She then hopes they will recommend her restaurant to the tourists."

"If her food is any good," added a gloomy Brian. He leaned from the chair and put his head down on the oak desk.

"My parents can't go so they gave the invitation to me. I'm allowed to take a friend."

Brian's head shot up. "A friend?"

"Yep, a friend." Sammy glanced at Joyce and winked. "Brian, it's too bad you don't think Alex's cooking is any good. That makes my choice easier."

"Hey, hey, wait a minute. I said, 'if.' " Brian grinned. "Her food could be good, you know."

Sammy winked again at Joyce. "No, no. The way she treated you at the restaurant window. I don't think I'm even going." He tossed the invitation on the desk.

"That's not the right attitude to take," said Brian, picking up the paper. "Here's a woman, on her own, working hard to start her own business and—" Brian glanced at the bottom of the invitation. After the "List the names of those attending," Sammy had written: Sammy Wilson, Brian Helm, and Joyce Myers.

Even though Joyce knew Sammy was kidding, she didn't fully understand the bewildered look on Brian's face.

Brian turned the paper toward Joyce and smiled. "He's taking both of us."

"When is this free meal?" asked Joyce, putting her rocker in gear and pushing full speed ahead.

"Day after tomorrow, six-thirty in the evening. Casual dress," replied Sammy.

"I'm game," said Joyce.

Brian shook his head. With a smirk he said, "I don't know. My calendar is pretty full. You know, my other social obligations. But I will sacrifice. What are friends for? Right, Sammy?"

Sammy said, "Good. We'll leave from here at six-fifteen."

Brian's comment, "What are friends for?" echoed in Sammy's head. He thought of George Brock who had been released from the hospital that afternoon. He remembered telling George that he and Brian were his friends. Some friends they were. Somebody out there was trying to kill George, and they hadn't been able to stop it. Was that person smarter than they were?

All Sammy needed was one good clue. He looked toward the photos and moved back to the bed. "Let's take another look at the photos," he said in a determined tone.

"What if the buggy that blew up was the stolen buggy?" asked Joyce as she lifted herself out of the rocker.

Sammy retrieved the Amishman-pulling-the-buggy picture from the bed. "That means the buggy was stolen for the purpose of killing Mr. Brock. And in the process of taking the buggy, the loose letters somehow spilled out. Which means the Amishman stole the buggy then used it to destroy Mr. Brock and his business."

"And the mysterious Amishman's motive?"

"To eliminate competition."

"Or maybe the buggy wasn't stolen at all," said Brian. "David Fisher used it to do away with his welding competitor."

Joyce picked up another photo showing the Amishman and the buggy. "Does that look like David Fisher?"

Brian moved in between the two and swiveled his head to examine both images. "Can't tell. Most of his face is away from the camera. And they all dress alike."

Sammy quickly snatched up the other two shots—the Amishman waving in through the window and the one showing him petting the dog. "But what you can see is part of a heavy black beard. It can't be David Fisher. His beard is light and thin. In fact, my uncle kids him about whether he's old enough to grow a beard."

The girl detective grabbed another picture. "This Amishman in the corn field has a heavy black beard. Could it be the same Amishman?"

For the first time that evening, the excitement started to build in the room. Three pairs of eyes strained to compare the likenesses. While the figure of the Amishman in back was much smaller, they made the comparison. Yes. They all agreed it could be the same man. It was the same straw hat, the same long-sleeved shirt, and black pants.

"Remember, after he petted the dog, he walked back up along the welding shop to the corn field."

"That's right," said Brian, pulling that particular snapshot from the bed. "It has to be the same man."

"Hey, wait a minute," said Sammy, who was inspecting the enlargement of the Amishman and the dog. "Looky here at what I see."

Brian knew by the way Sammy had said it, that he had found a vital clue. "What?" asked Brian as he searched the black and white photo.

"When the Amishman reached over to pet the dog, his arm extended out from his sleeve. Look, it's a watch. The Amishman is wearing a wrist watch."

"So," said Brian.

"The Amish don't wear wrist watches," said Joyce. "Their religion doesn't allow them to wear jewelry of any kind. That includes watches."

"Which means our Amishman here is not an Amishman," stated Sammy proudly. "Somebody dressed up as an Amishman to disguise himself."

"So we're right back where we started," said Brian. "It could be anybody."

"No, it couldn't," returned Sammy. "There's another clue in that picture that points to a certain kind of person."

"He's left-handed," said Joyce. "See, he's petting the dog with his left hand."

"Right," said Sammy, and he immediately pictured each suspect, one by one. He remembered in what hand Barry Bitner held the tire iron. He pictured Jack Mills wiping the raindrops from his glasses. He saw Wally Mills sticking the lollipop into his mouth. He recalled how, months earlier, Charlie Gordon had stepped up into the plane and then extended his hand to help Brian and him inside. He saw Alex Austin moving her hand over the quilts. He visualized how David Fisher had handled the business cards.

Brian was watching his friend. "You're latching onto something, aren't you. We're not at a dead end anymore. Right, Sammy?"

Sammy's gaze traveled up the arm to the camera-shy face of the would-be Amishman. "There's only one person involved in this case that's left-handed," he said.

"Yeah, that's me," said Brian, holding up and waving his left hand.

"No, there's another person who's also left-handed. Now we have to prove he's responsible for the explosion." Sammy hurried to his desk and sat facing the computer. With it on, he clicked the icon. The list and information about each suspect that he had entered appeared on the monitor.

Brian and Joyce waited, giving Sammy time and space to spin the web that would entrap Mr. Bomber.

When he was finished reviewing the information, Sammy leaned back in his chair and smiled. "Okay, here's what we're going to do. Joyce, tomorrow morning, go to Alex Austin's restaurant and find out who's going to be at the buffet dinner. I'm sure Charlie Gordon will not be invited. But I think Mr. Brock will be on the list.

If Jack and Wally Mills, Barry Bitner, and David Fisher are not listed, ask Alex to do us a favor and invite them."

"In other words," said Joyce, "do whatever is necessary to get our suspects to that dinner."

"Right. And can you enlarge the photo to give detail to the watch?"

Joyce looked again at the print. "Sure, no problem."

"And Brian, you find Barry Bitner and convince him that he should attend the free meal if he is invited. I don't think he'll need much persuasion. Judging from his size, he must enjoy eating."

The plan was still whirling around in Sammy's head. He was hoping to have some insight to insure the plan would work. He got up and went to the window and gazed at the darkening sky. His face was relaxed as he turned and faced his two friends. "Let's plan to meet with Detective Ben Phillips at the police station tomorrow afternoon at three."

"And what is our fearless leader going to be doing while Joyce and I are out beating the bushes?"

"I will be at the Smoketown airport, checking on Charlie Gordon," said Sammy. "I want to see if he's capable of holding a bomb in his hands."

"What kind of bomb?" asked Joyce.

Sammy produced a big grin. "The kind that, when it goes off, says, 'I got ya!'"

CHAPTER TWELVE

Normally at three o'clock in the afternoon, Detective Phillips was busy doing paper work. The only thing that kept him from filling out forms today was the bombing. He was busy collecting information.

A stack of folders loomed in front of him as he shifted in his chair. The files contained background checks on the suspects and the preliminary test results from the lab. He closed and tossed the last one on top of the others. He took a deep breath, leaned back, and interlocked his fingers behind his head. He was glad that was over. Reading about the troubles and hardships of others depressed him.

The three teenagers on bikes, riding past his window, caught his attention. He smiled for the first time that day. "Hey, Marvin," he yelled out the open door, "can I have another folding chair for my office. I'm getting company."

Detective Marvin Wetzel appeared with the chair. "Where're you going to put it? On top of your desk?"

Without saying anything, Ben grabbed the coffee table and pulled it past Marvin and out into the hallway. He returned and sat again behind his desk. "Put the chair there. I'll do without coffee for the next hour."

Marvin deposited the chair where the table had been. "You know, Ben, if you weren't in this room, the room would be ten times bigger." He smiled and dashed back to his own office next door.

No one was more pleased to see the third chair than Brian. Before, when Joyce was with them, there had only been two chairs and he had had to stand. It reminded Brian of school. When you were bad you had to stand in the corner. And Phillips' office was small. No matter where you stood, you were practically in a corner.

"Well, do you know who done it?" asked Phillips, half kidding, as the trio squeezed into the chairs.

Brian was in a corner, but at least he was *sitting* in the corner. He smiled and said, "Show him the pictures, Joyce."

Joyce placed two photographs on the desk beside the folders. The top photo showed an Amishman petting a dog. The one underneath was an enlargement of just the arm petting the dog.

The detective picked up the prints, one in each hand. His penetrating eyes didn't miss a detail. "Hum, both made from the same negative." He glanced at Sammy. "Now, what kind of Amishman wears a watch?"

"None that I know of," answered the teenager.

"Right. So our Amishman isn't an Amishman. I'm going to have to put you three on the payroll. This is good detective work."

Brian produced a grin then lost it. "But none of the pictures shows his face enough to identify him."

"That's too bad," said Phillips. "But we do know that this person is responsible for the bombing. I just finished looking over these reports. Dynamite was in the buggy when it exploded. The lab found gunpowder residue on pieces of material from the buggy seat."

Sammy stood. "I need to know one thing before I can answer the first question you asked as we came in. Do they know yet how the dynamite was detonated?"

"Yep," said Phillips, leaning back in his chair. "Remote control."

"That's what I thought," said Sammy. "And the answer to your question is—yes, I know who did it. Thanks to Joyce and Brian."

Phillips quickly inquired, "Can you prove it?"

"No, but..."

"You have a plan," added Phillips.

"Sammy always has a plan. Right, Sammy?"

"We know his plan has something to do with the free buffet at Alex's restaurant," said Joyce.

Phillips opened a desk drawer. "I lucked out. I happened to be at the front door of the station when Alex Austin arrived. So guess who's going to represent the police department at her celebration?" he said, producing the invitation.

Joyce's face lit up. "Yeah, I saw your name on the list."

Detective Phillips looked puzzled. Then he frowned. "I guess you already have the plan in progress. Mind letting me in on it?"

"First, with your help, we need to pick up some evidence," said Sammy, heading for the door. "I'll explain my plan on the way."

CHAPTER THIRTEEN

B rian was developing a plan of his own as he gawked at the variety of food displayed on the long table. This evening couldn't have come soon enough. And now that it was here, he was ready. No rolls, he thought to himself, they're too filling. I want to fill up with the good stuff, like.... His glanced at the far end of the table. Pie, cake...chocolate-covered strawberries. He must be dreaming.

Joyce snapped her elbow into Brian's side and startled him. "That's the dessert end of the table. That's for later. Come on, you're holding up the line."

Brian looked around and saw heads bending this way and that, all watching him. He mumbled something to himself, grabbed a fork, and started to pile slices of roast beef onto his plate. He stopped when Joyce again nudged him with her elbow. Next he scooped mashed potatoes and used the bottom of the spoon to make a cavity. The gravy spilled over the potatoes and beef and gave the plate a brown bottom. He wrinkled his nose at the peas and corn. But there was room on the plate for more even if it had to sit in the gravy. He plopped a small mound of baked beans into the pool of brown. As he hurried back to the booth, he eyed the chocolate-covered strawberries.

Sammy was in line behind Joyce. Because guests were still arriving, he glanced at the individuals being greeted at the door by Alex Austin. Everything had not gone as planned. This was real life, not television. The search yesterday had not produced the crucial piece of evidence that would have canceled today's activity. Now his plan was needed to trap the guilty person. He selected some salad, ham with pineapple, a baked potato, and lima beans, and followed Joyce to their booth.

"Boy, you're hard at it. What's the rush?" asked Joyce as she slid in next to Brian.

He ignored her question and gave a quick glance at her plate. "Salad. Is that all you're eating? Why fill up with salad when you can have all the other good stuff?" He shoved a slice of beef into his mouth and said something that sounded like, "Hey, it's free."

"Yeah, but the visit to the doctor's office isn't free," said Joyce. "The key to eating food is to eat slowly. That way you have time to taste it, chew it, and digest it."

Sammy's face lit up in reaction to something Joyce had said. He was remembering something. Something he had seen. Yes! Yes! He now had the missing piece to the puzzle.

Brian noticed the smile on Sammy's face. He pointed with his empty fork. "So you saw the chocolate-covered strawberries over there?"

"Yeah, high class," said Sammy, feeling just super.

"Mind if I join you?" said a familiar voice.

Sammy looked up. "No, I was saving this seat for you, Mr. Brock."

He sat next to Sammy. "Most people here don't want me sitting near them. After two years, you'd think they'd forget and forgive."

"How are you doing, Mr. Brock?" asked Joyce sincerely. "Any aches or pains?"

"No, I was lucky. Being inside that feed hopper was better than wearing a suit of armor. It saved my life."

"But your welding business is destroyed," added Sammy. "Did you have any insurance on it?"

"A little. Enough to rebuild, I hope." George Brock looked around. "What do I have to do to get some food?"

Brian backed the fork away from his mouth, turned his head, and nodded. "Over there. Grab a plate and fill up."

George got up. "Wow, I see they have—"

"Yeah," said Joyce, "but Brian has his name on them."

George shrugged and smiled. "That's okay. I'll eat them anyway, as long as his name's written in chocolate."

"Save ten for me," said Brian.

At that point a booming voice erupted from the next booth. "No, you don't. Those chocolate strawberries are mine."

The three looked in surprise (about fifty if you count the others who heard the pronouncement). A serious face showed itself over the back of the booth. The mouth then curved into a smile as did the thin mustache above it. The eyes were yet to be heard from.

Brian's guilt sprang into words. "Hi, Detective Phillips. How are you doing? Getting enough to eat? Boy, I am. I can't eat another bite."

"I'm not just here to eat, Brian," said Phillips. "I'm here as a security guard to make sure everybody takes only one chocolate-covered strawberry." He looked, allowing his eyes to address the room. Then he roared with laugher.

When he laughed, so did the others in the restaurant, especially Alex Austin. It was at this point that all the guests seemed to bond socially. Instead of individuals enjoying themselves, they were now a group with something in common. At least for the next several minutes, each table and booth would be having chocolate-covered strawberries in their conversation.

Sammy felt what David Fisher had hinted at days earlier. Every other Sunday, Amish families came together for church service, ate side by side, and shared their tales of the last two weeks and their plans for the next two. However, the plans he had set in motion for this social would not have the Amish seal of approval.

The restaurant could seat sixty-six people. And since sixty-six guests were invited, they had to share the booths and tables. Wally and Jack Mills were at a table getting acquainted with Bob and Genny LoBianco. The LoBiancos were new to the area and operated Genny's Specialty Cottage.

Barry Bitner was busy eating but was listening to a story being told by Anne from the bookstore. Bob Good, the postmaster, shared a table with Jake Bare of the Bare Potato Company, Fred Steudler of Val Products, and Mel Horst of the Folkcraft Museum. Conversation, mixed with laughter, rippled through the restaurant.

Nora and Jennifer, two blond waitresses, moved among the guests, removing empty plates and serving drinks. They were business-like as they, too, wanted this party to be successful.

Twenty minutes later, when most of the guests were trying to find room for dessert, a lone figure slipped in unnoticed through the side entrance. He made his way toward Sammy's booth.

Gifts of flowers, plants, aprons, and potholders had been presented to Alex by some of the guests. Now Charlie Gordon brought something. Something very special. It was strapped to his chest.

No one seemed to notice Charlie Gordon until he had planted his feet directly beside George Brock.

Sammy, Brian, Joyce, and George looked up at the misshapen figure before them. They had a feeling that the party was over.

"I have a bomb! Nobody move!" Charlie yelled. Sticks of dynamite were fastened to his upper body. A six-volt battery had complex wiring that roamed over and around the dynamite.

Everybody gasped.

Detective Ben Phillips in the next booth turned his head slowly and glanced up. He saw a face of a scared but determined man. He felt the weight of his own gun strapped against his body.

Charlie leaned against George Brock. "Nobody move or I'll blow us all up!"

But someone did move. Alex took two steps toward her ex-boyfriend. "Charlie, don't do this."

"Stop right there, love, or your clean boyfriend here will get a little messy."

George, who was giving his whole attention to the bomb, reacted quickly while Charlie was glancing at Alex. He grabbed and raised Charlie's right arm and at the same time yanked the green wire from among the others on Charlie's chest.

"What the— What did you do?" screamed Charlie.

Detective Phillips slipped his gun from under his left arm and swung around. He pointed his revolver, not at Charlie Gordon, but at George Brock.

Charlie stepped back away from the booth as Phillips jumped up and replaced him.

"A lot of people would have been scared to do what you just did, George," said Phillips. "Especially someone like you who just went through a traumatic bombing experience. How do you explain that, George?"

"I don't know," answered George. "It was reflex I guess."

"But you knew to raise Charlie's right arm up and away from the firing button. You also pulled out the green wire. That was the only wire that could disarm the bomb."

Sammy, sitting next to George, said, "Maybe it was something you were trained to do in Vietnam. Is that the reflex you meant?"

George Brock glanced down at the chocolate-covered strawberry he didn't get to eat. He slowly stole a side glance at Detective Phillips who was blocking his exit from the booth. He could feel the eyes of the stunned locals, sitting with their unfinished desserts before them. George had been in tougher spots than this. His mouth twisted to the side. His gaze returned to Sammy. "Vietnam was a long time ago. To me it's a long forgotten story."

"Well, let me tell you a more recent story," said Sammy. "A welder's wife left him. In his grief, he accidentally killed another man's wife in an automobile accident. His friends and neighbors turned against him. Business people stopped buying his iron crafts. He had a lot of time and money invested in his unsold merchandise. His business was going nowhere. Ah, but the welding shop and goods were insured for three hundred thousand dollars. However, if the shop was destroyed, the police surely would suspect foul play. So what could he do to throw suspicion away from himself?"

Brock's mouth turned up into a cunning smile.

Sammy continued. "He developed this clever plan. Since the cinder-block building and wrought iron crafts couldn't be destroyed easily by fire, he would use dynamite. After all, with his years in the armed service, he knew how to construct a bomb. Now comes the clever part. He would make it appear that his life was in danger. That he was receiving threatening notes and phone calls. That there were people out there who wanted to kill him—*in his welding shop.* Later, when an attempt is made on his life in the welding shop, no one would suspect the real reason for the bombing. And that was to destroy the building, the equipment, the overstock, and to collect the insurance money."

"It's nonsense, absolute nonsense," said Brock. "If that's true, why did I have you three protect me?"

"Witnesses, Mr. Brock," said Sammy. "Your plan needed witnesses, somebody to see someone other than yourself plant the bomb. When Detective Phillips suggested you contact two teenagers to help you, we fell right into your plan. We would be the witnesses you needed."

"But I was threatened," pleaded Brock. "You saw the guy running from my shop after he had left that note."

"No, we didn't see anybody. You pretended to see someone running away from your shop when we drove there. Then while Brian and I ran to investigate, you either wrote the threatening note or you already had it written."

"And you stole the buggy," added Brian. He raised two chocolate-smeared fingers. "You stole the buggy for two reasons. One, as a way to transport and conceal the bomb. And two, as a cover for your disguise as an Amishman."

"But I was in my shop when the Amishman and the buggy arrived."

Sammy nodded at Joyce sitting across from him. "Joyce, do you want to tell him how he can be in two places at once?"

"I can tell him how he could *appear* to be in two places at the same time. By the time Dottie arrived with the chicken barbecue, you had already left by the back door. You changed into your Amish clothes back among the trees. From our vantage point across the creek, we couldn't see you."

"But I was welding the feed hopper and didn't hear Dottie knock at the door."

Joyce ignored George's comment and continued. "After you were dressed as the Amishman, you came out from behind the trees and stood awhile. You wanted to make sure we saw you from across the creek. You then walked along the edge of the corn field and out of the picture. You really went the back way to your house up the road or to wherever the buggy was hidden. Next, you pulled the buggy down the road to your shop in full view of us, your witnesses. And then just to enrich the illusion, you went to the window and waved, making us believe the 'Amishman' was waving to the welder inside. You then walked around back, entered the trees, changed from the Amish clothes into your own, and came down through the blind spot and into your shop."

"That makes a good story," said Brock. "But that's all it is—a story. You can't prove anything." He put his hands on the table, leaned forward, and started to stand.

Detective Phillips rested his gun on top of Brock's head and pushed downward. Brock reluctantly stayed seated.

"But we do have proof," said Brian. "We always have proof before we accuse anyone of a crime. Right, Sammy?"

"Those cut-out letters you dropped at the carriage shop," said Sammy. "I'm guessing they fell from your shirt pocket when you stooped over to pick up the buggy shafts. You had intended to glue the letters on paper and present it as another threat on your life."

"You can't prove that those pieces of paper belonged to me. Anybody could have dropped them."

Sammy shook his head. "After the explosion, before they took you to the hospital, you repeated their message, word for word. You said, 'You will die in your shop.' Then you scoffed at the idea, pretending you had cheated death." Sammy tapped his fingers on the table. "Only the person who cut out those letters to send himself a death threat could know the message they contained."

"When you told me you had solved the secret of the letters, you repeated the message."

"No, I didn't. I just said their message was the same as the others. I did not tell you the exact wording."

The color drained from Brock's face. His body went limp. He wasn't prepared for what was happening to him.

"May I see your keys, Mr. Brock?" asked Sammy.

Brock gave a sigh of relief. "So you do know," he said as he reached for his keys and gave them to Sammy.

Sammy pointed his finger at Joyce Myers. "It really started with her photos. Once I suspected it was you, the rest of the pieces fell into place.

The police lab report said the bomb was detonated by remote control. You were in the feed hopper when the bomb went off. So the remote had to be somewhere in the feed hopper. Yesterday we inspected every piece of equipment that was with you in the bin. And we found nothing."

"Pretty smart, huh?" said Brock.

Joyce shook her head, "What's smart about going to jail?"

"The missing remote had me stumped until Joyce used the word 'key.' I remembered you dropped your set of keys before you were put into the ambulance. And when they were handed back to you, I noticed something." Sammy held up the keys.

"What do those keys have to do with the bombing?" asked Brian.

"It's not the keys," explained Sammy. "It's this." Sammy pointed to the black key ring holder which held the keys. It was about two inches long, an inch and a half wide, and a half-inch thick. "This is a remote control unit that transmits a radio signal to lock and unlock car doors."

The young detective dangled the black plastic rectangle in front of George Brock. "This remote certainly isn't for your old truck, is it Mr. Brock?"

Brock shook his head. He had had enough. "No, you're right. I used it to detonate the bomb. The detective here was right. You kids are smart."

Sammy handed the remote and the keys to Detective Phillips. Then to reassure himself of the facts, Sammy said, "You made the iron hopper especially for the bombing. It was to protect you during the explosion. After you pushed the button, and the building was blowing apart, you shoved the remote control unit with its keys into your pocket. Then it was just a matter of lying down and waiting to be rescued."

"You almost got away with your scheme," added Phillips. "But your downfall came when, dressed as the Amishman, you stopped to pet the dog."

George shook his head. "You knew it was me because I petted the dog?"

"You used your left hand when you stroked the dog. When you did, your shirt sleeve pulled up and exposed your wrist watch."

"And the Amish don't wear wrist watches," said Brock in a monotone. "But—"

Brian was anxious to butt in again. "You and I are the only ones in this case that are left-handed. Right, Sammy?"

"Because of the watch, I knew the Amishman was not Amish," said Sammy. "Because of the crime lab report, I knew the buggy was the source of the bomb. So it had to be a left-handed 'Englishman' who constructed the bomb."

"But how did—?"

"Your golf clubs," said Sammy. "When Brian was trying out your nine iron, he mentioned that it was made for him, a perfect fit. Brian is left-handed and so are you, Mr. Brock. All the suspects are right-handed."

"But that doesn't prove—"

"No, it doesn't prove you did it," said Phillips. "But this remote control, along with your confession, does. Also our background check turned up that you were assigned to a demolition unit in Vietnam. The skill you displayed here with Charlie demonstrates that you are knowledge-able enough about explosives to construct a bomb and explode it."

"Why?" asked Joyce. "Why did you do it?"

Brock peered out at the faces of those who were members of the business community. Some faces reflected embarrassment for him. Others showed scorn. George pointed past Detective Phillips. His words of denial suddenly changed to words of hate. "It's because of them that I did it. Just once, I wanted them to see me as a victim. Just once I wanted them to feel sorry for me." He said it loud enough for all to hear. Then he looked at the fifteen-year-old girl sitting opposite him. "Do you know what it's like to live in a town where most of the people hate you? They turned against me. And just because of one human mistake."

Joyce shook her head but said nothing.

"Most of the people we talked to," said Brian, "told us they felt sorry for you."

"Then why did welding jobs stop coming my way? Why did vendors stop buying my crafts?"

"Maybe because you stopped believing in yourself," said Sammy. "Maybe the person who turned against you the most was yourself. Being responsible for someone's death is a lot of guilt to carry. Your attitude changed. Your work habits changed. As you were building up your plan to collect the insurance money and leave town, your business was going down hill."

Brock lowered his head. "I didn't want to hurt anybody. That's why I wanted you three across the creek when the dynamite exploded. I knew from that distance you wouldn't be injured from the blast."

"And what about Barry Bitner?" asked Sammy. "Did you want to hurt him?"

"Well, he's different. He's a troublemaker."

"How is Barry different? He didn't steal pieces of iron from you, did he?"

Brock hung his head "No, he didn't. I needed someone else to blame for the threats."

The room went quiet.

Phillips moved the gun butt away from Brock's head. With his left hand he guided George out from the booth. "George Brock, you're under arrest for the bombing of your welding shop." He led his prisoner out the side door, reading him his rights as they headed for the police car.

Charlie Gordon, who had been all too willing to help in Sammy's entrapment plan, thought it best to leave also. Maybe after things settled down, Alex might give him another chance.

Sammy slid out of the booth and stood, facing the guests. "You just heard that Barry didn't steal anything from Mr. Brock. Last month, Barry thought the wood he took was being thrown away. Every time something bad happens, people are ready to blame Barry Bitner. Barry has no police record of any kind. The only bad thing Barry has is a temper. And you, too, might have a temper if people accused you every time some trouble appeared."

Barry was stunned. All of a sudden he was the center of attention. Sammy had done everything except put a halo above his head. Barry produced a sheepish smile and lowered his head. This was one time he didn't have to defend himself.

Sammy didn't know Barry could look so humble. Before the mood was broken, Sammy said, "Barry's a good worker, and I hear he's looking for a job. I bet one of you business people might just have a job opening for him. How about it? Let's see some hands out there."

Four hands went up.

Sammy smiled. "Barry, it looks like you're needed. Now it's up to you. Good luck."

Alex joined the trio as Joyce and Brian slid out from the booth. "That was a nice thing you did for Barry, Sammy."

"Thank you," said Sammy. "Barry has had enough dumped on him. I thought it was necessary for all of us to hear and understand how our attitudes toward ourselves and others can affect lives. Because of what we witnessed here this evening, maybe we can show more compassion toward each other."

"Yeah, Mr. Brock's attitude didn't do him any good," added Brian. "And I bet Barry's attitude gave him his temper. Right, Sammy? What is attitude anyway?"

"I guess it's the way we think about things and how we decide to respond to them."

Sammy's remarks reminded Alex of something. "I want to apologize to you boys for the way I acted before. My attitude this last month has been bad."

"Hey, you've been under a lot of pressure," said Sammy. "It's not easy to open a business like this."

"You don't know the half of it," said Alex. "When I was trying to get a business loan, I was frequently told, 'A man never made a go of a restaurant there. What makes you think as a woman you can?' That remark made me even more determined to make this restaurant work."

Joyce motioned toward the guests still eating or milling about. "They'll help you get the word out."

"They're nice people," said Alex. "Oh, and, Joyce, I did what you suggested. As everybody came in this evening, I told everyone, except George Brock, of course, of our attempt at a little dinner theater. I told them to act scared at the mention of a bomb."

"They did a great job," said Sammy.

Alex smiled and pointed to a corner table. "I just talked to Sonny Longenecker, the barber, and his two daughters. They said that they didn't have to act, they really were scared. The setting was too real."

"Speaking of setting," said Joyce, "what happened to the Amish quilt and buggy you were going to display?"

"This area already has an Amish theme," said Alex. "I don't need to add to it. I decided instead to keep the restaurant plain and simple. I'll serve top quality steaks along with generous helpings."

Sammy stepped closer to Alex and lowered his voice. "Thanks for allowing us to use your restaurant for our little charade. You were a good sport to do it, and the food was great."

"It'll be good for business," said Alex. "They'll be talking about it for weeks."

"I know they'll be talking about your straw-berries," said Brian, grinning.

"Yes, *somebody* enjoyed them. They're all gone," kidded Alex, staring at Brian's chocolate-rimmed smile.

"Well, gang, we'd better be gone, too," said Sammy. "We're finished here."

"Good-bye," they all said and headed for the door.

"Well, Brian," said Sammy, "do you still think this case was dumb?"

"No, I changed my mind," said Brian. "The case was not dumb. It was delicious." He held up something in his hand and said, "Hey, it would have been thrown away anyway." He popped the very last chocolate-covered strawberry into his mouth.

The very last.

The one George Brock didn't get to eat.

SAMMY AND BRIAN MYSTERY SERIES

#1 The Quilted Message by Ken Munro
The whole village was talking about it. Did the Amish quilt contain more than just twenty mysterious cloth pictures? The pressure was on for Bird-in-Hand's two teenage detectives, Sammy and Brian, to solve the mystery. Was Amos King murdered because of the quilt? Who broke into the country store? It was time for Sammy and Brian to unmask the intruder. $4.95

#2 Bird in the Hand by Ken Munro
When arson is suspected on an Amish farm, the village of Bird-in-Hand responds with a fund-raiser. The appearance of a mysterious tattooed man starts a series of events that ends in murder. And who is The Bird? Sammy and Brian are bound hand and foot by the feathered creature. Bird-in-Hand's own teenage sleuths break free and unravel the mystery. $5.95

#3 Amish Justice by Ken Munro
The duo turns into a trio when Joyce Myers becomes the newest member of the Sammy and Brian detective team. Is farmland in Lancaster County worth killing for? Frank Crawford thinks so. And when the police call the attempts on his life accidents, the old farmer sends for the teenage detectives. The three sleuths soon discover one of five suspects knows about the "IT" under the house. . . $5.95

#4 Jonathan's Journal by Ken Munro
After Scott Boyer comes to town, a young girl disappears. He then makes an offer Sammy and Brian can't refuse. A 200-year-old journal holds a challenge of a lifetime. It holds two secrets: a mysterious puzzle and murder. Bird-in-Hand's super detectives investigate the meaning behind its cryptic message. $5.95

#5 Doom Buggy by Ken Munro
An Amish buggy disappears. Twenty cut-out letters appear in its place. Then someone wants George Brock dead—in his welding shop. Sammy, Brian, and Joyce, fifteen-year-old sleuths from Bird-in-Hand, try to find the connection between these three mysterious happenings. $5.95

— —

These books may be purchased at your local bookstore or ordered from Gaslight Publishers, P. O. Box 258, Bird-in-Hand, PA 17505.

Enclosed is $_____(please add $2.00 for shipping and handling). Send check or money order only.

Name _____

Address _____

City _____ State _____ Zip _____